The Kidnapping of Taylor Shaw
Tighe Taylor, JD

Copyright © 2022 Tighe Taylor, JD

All rights reserved. No part of this book may be reproduced or transmitted in any form or by any means, electronic or mechanical, including photocopying, recording or by any information storage and retrieval system without permission in writing from the publisher.

Black Cat Publishing—Sherman Oaks, CA
ISBN: 979-8-218-04891-4
Library of Congress Control Number: 2022914248
Title: The Kidnapping of Taylor Shaw
Author: Tighe Taylor, JD
Digital distribution | 2022
Paperback | 2022

This is a work of fiction. The characters, names, incidents, places, and dialogue are products of the author's imagination, and are not to be construed as real.

Previous books by Tighe Taylor

The Tragic Death of Marina Habe
The Kidnapping of Tammy Fitzgerald

Chapter One
Sacramento, California

It was pitch black outside. Three 18 wheelers rumbled down the highway towards a 12-foot high double gate in the equally high chain link fence that surrounded the yard.

The lead vehicle stopped at the gate. The other two fell in behind. The driver of the lead vehicle jumped down from the cab with a large bolt cutter. He cut the lock, pulled the chain out, and opened the gate creating an opening for the large trucks.

He returned to his vehicle, and all three trucks passed through the gate and into the yard. All three turned around and backed their rear doors in the direction of a large earthen area.

From each vehicle, a driver and three passengers jumped down to the ground. One passenger from each was left to guard his vehicle.

The remaining men opened the rear cargo doors and began removing drums which appeared to hold liquid waste.

Some drums from previous deliveries were already present at the site and were being stored on an earth-covered area near the proposed dumping site. Waste could be seen seeping from the stored drums and into the surrounding ground.

It appears as if the men were directed to pour the contents of the drums just delivered as well as the contents of the drums stored on the property into the large earthen basin. Judging from the size of the trucks, it appeared as if the illegal dumping operation was being carried on by a very large company.

From a tip, the enforcement division of the California Environmental Protection Agency was able to find the location. This made it possible for them to set up in a nearby abandoned building before the illegal activity commenced. The hope was to catch them in the act. The operation was being carried out by the Office of Criminal Investigation (OCI) of the California Department of Toxic Substance Control.

The OCI brass was observing from the third floor of the abandoned building many feet away. The building was rented by the State of California for the operation.

Taylor Shaw, wearing a bulky OCI jacket over dark blue slacks and a business-like light blue blouse, was among the observers. She was the only woman. They were in one room with blacked-out windows. She was there being evaluated for a position with the California EPA task force within the State Attorney General's Office and was asked to observe along with a few other candidates and OCI officers.

She was already working for the State Attorney General in the Fairview office, primarily in elder abuse.

She was thinking to herself that her husband, Rick, was right. She would be promoted from elder abuse to white collar crimes within a year. The only problem was that as part of the white-collar crimes task force, she would not be allowed to share the nature of all of her duties with anyone, including her husband, and that would be very difficult. She and Rick kept no secrets from one another. That is just how their relationship operated.

She was very excited about her possible new position and thought to herself that she was ready to undertake her new duties. She was confident that Rick would support her, as he had always supported her decisions in the past.

The OCI observers were looking out over the yard and the activities of the several men who arrived to do the unloading. It appeared as if the men were ordered to conduct their activities only after no one else was at the facility and only after dark.

The liquid waste being delivered appeared to be chemical waste which was a byproduct of chemical manufacturing.

The senior OCI observers determined that the disposal plan was in place and ready for execution. Just as the dumping began, enormous stadium lights magically came on lighting the yard as if it were daytime. Three helicopters quickly came into the air space above the yard. Three step-up vans delivered three platoons of armed OCI officers dressed in riot gear and carrying automatic weapons. They exited the vans spread out into the yard.

At that time, the leader of the OCI team raised a bullhorn and delivered the following message to the perpetrators: "This is the enforcement division of the California Environmental Protection

Agency. You are completely surrounded by units of armed officers and your movements are being watched from three helicopters flying above. Please stop whatever you are doing, lay down any weapons you may have, and prepare to be taken into custody. Please do not re-enter your vehicles."

From the observation room, the entire affair played out like an action movie on steroids. Taylor was thinking to herself that she had never seen such a display of force, even in a movie.

The OCI team moved in. The twelve perpetrators were so comprehensively surrounded that they had their hands up and were down on their knees even before being asked to do so.

Taylor was riveted. This was the most excitement that she experienced in years, and, frankly, she loved it.

The perpetrators were handcuffed and taken away in official vehicles to be processed and questioned.

Several staff people remained to evaluate the scene.

As some liquid waste had seeped out of the drums and into the ground, an inspection was made to determine what methods could be used to remediate the area to attempt to clean up the toxic substance and to prevent it from seeping further.

One inspector conducted dye testing of a nearby storm drain. Fluorescein dye was placed into the drain opening. By adding water, the dye would be conducted to the outfall of the drain where it could be seen unloading into its destination.

It was determined that this storm drain unloaded collected liquid into the nearby Cherokee River. This meant that the river, its banks, and any wells supplied by it would have to be remediated.

The OCI observers and the task force candidates left the observation room. As it was now quite late, the candidates were asked by Mr. Deaver, the EPA's liaison, to return to his Sacramento office the next day at 10 o'clock in the morning.

Earlier in the day, Taylor and the other candidates met with Mr. Deaver to receive instructions as to how and when they would meet to be transported to the observation area. This would be late at night, under cover of darkness, with no fanfare, and without drawing attention to the operation. The reasons were painfully obvious.

An OCI vehicle took Taylor and the other candidates back to their rental cars which were parked at the Attorney General's office.

Taylor drove to her hotel room, slept, had breakfast, and returned to the AG's office the next morning, arriving at 10 a.m., as requested.

Chapter Two
The Sacramento Office of the Attorney General of the State of California

The Sacramento office of the State Attorney General was nondescript. It was housed in a typical multi-story glass office building. There were 175 square foot offices with windows around the perimeter of the building with views of downtown Sacramento. The corner offices were larger. In the hallway immediately outside of the perimeter offices, there were secretarial bays. The look was much the same as a typical law office suite.

There were a couple of large interior spaces used as conference rooms. Today's meeting would be held in one of these rooms.

When Taylor arrived at the office, she was directed to Conference Room A. The room had no windows and a large table in its center. She was directed to take a seat at the table. When admission to the room was complete, there were a total of 6 people, including Taylor, Mr. Deaver, and four additional candidates for the task force.

All six of the people in the meeting were in the observation room the previous night. Introductions in the observation room were brief.

This meeting today was led by Mr. Deaver. He was a man of about 50, in the prime of his professional life. He was gray around the temples, but appeared to keep himself in pretty good shape. He was good looking for his age. He wore a wedding ring and had the earmarks of a family man.

He addressed the group with the following:

Hello everyone, my name is John Deaver. I briefly met all of you yesterday both here and in the observation room last night.

I am with the Attorney General in Sacramento and am the liaison with the EPA's enforcement division.

Let's go around the room and have everyone introduce him or herself. We will start here to my left and go clockwise around the table. What is your name sir?

The first person to his left gave his name as David Samuels. He said he was from San Diego. The next person gave his name as Jerry Flack. He said he was from Los Angeles. The next person gave his name as Eric Vandyke. He said he was from San Francisco. The next person gave his name as Thomas Sullivan. He said he was from Redding.

Taylor was the next person, sitting immediately to Mr. Deaver's right. She told the group that her name was Taylor Shaw and that she was from Fairview, a suburb of Bryan. She said that it is in the California desert in the vicinity of Palm Springs.

Mr. Deaver said that as chief liaison, he worked out of the main office in Sacramento, where we were meeting.

Mr. Deaver continued his talk. He said that he wanted to give us a quick refresher course about the Environmental Protection Agency to help us better understand our mission. He started with the State of California.

On the State level, in 1961, Governor Edmund G. Brown, Sr. oversaw the reorganization of the executive branch of the State of California.

When his son, Governor Edmund G. ("Jerry") Brown, Jr. took office in 1975, the junior Governor Brown proposed a separate State agency dedicated to the environment. When this idea was turned down, the junior Governor Brown settled for the establishment of a new cabinet level position known as the Secretary of Environmental Affairs.

In 1991, under Governor Pete Wilson, the California EPA was established.

Today, the California EPA, known as CalEPA, consists of several departments which oversee such things as clean air, clean water, toxic substances, and environmental hazards.

On the federal level, in 1970, the Environmental Protection Agency (EPA) was formed under President Nixon.

The Clean Air Act and the Clean Water Act, both enacted in 1970, advised the EPA to set standards for clean air, clean water, and suitable toxic waste disposal.

The plan was for Congress to enact environment laws setting forth its broad desires and for the EPA to promulgate regulations concerning enforcement by administrative action, civil action, or criminal prosecution.

There continues to be some overlapping between CalEPA and the federal EPA. As time has progressed, however, the federal EPA has become more interested in violations on federal lands and with emergencies, while CalEPA has become more concerned with violations within the State of California.

In California, in response to environmental disasters, the Department of Toxic Substances Control (DTSC) was placed under Cal EPA.

The DTSC developed its own enforcement arm, the Office of Criminal Investigations or OCI. Its investigators are duly sworn peace officers of the State of California. In addition to investigations, its members are authorized to make arrests and to carry firearms.

We were working with the OCI last night.

Generally speaking, the federal EPA looks to the Department of Justice and the U.S. Attorney's Office for prosecutions.

Generally speaking, CalEPA looks primarily to the State Attorney General (our office) and to the local District Attorneys for enforcement.

Mr. Deaver told us that we were here today to assist the State. We would be asked to help evaluate claims and tips concerning environmental violations and crimes which were being carried on primarily within the State.

The federal EPA maintains a National Response Center with an 800 number to report emergency environmental violations. CalEPA does not maintain an emergency response center and does not generally respond to emergencies.

CalEPA is more interested in investigating violations which are witnessed and reported such as ground water pollution, storm water runoff, wastewater discharge, solid waste transportation, improper storage, air quality and pesticide violations, and the illegal disposal of toxic substances.

Under certain circumstances, CalEPA will offer its Department of Toxic Substances Control to the federal EPA.

Taylor could not contain herself any longer. She asked, "Mr. Deaver, wouldn't it be more cost effective for a business to continue to pollute and just pay the fines?"

He replied, "That is a good question. Certainly, at one time, that may have been the case. However, as time has passed, the laws have progressed to include criminal sanctions, increased in fines, and the possible imprisonment of corporate officers. These provisions have added teeth to the older laws making violation and payment of fines a much less attractive option. It is one thing to pay a fine and go on about your business, but it is another thing to be criminally prosecuted, have a criminal record, and run the risk of cooling your heels in jail."

Taylor continued, "That is all well and good in the abstract, but maybe not in practice. In a recent case in Los Angeles, in response to an environmental law violation, a local company was allowed to demolish its plant and clean up its facility without criminal charges being filed. The company went into bankruptcy and did not even pay the cost of the cleanup, and there was no criminal conviction on which to rely as backup.

"While the deal was still pending, the lack of criminal sanctions made the case so obviously flawed that the federal EPA flew to Los Angeles to try to stop its consummation.

"The U.S. Attorney's Office for the Central District of California made more similar deals with corporations than were made in any of the other 93 U.S. Attorney offices throughout the country.

"It looks to me as if non-prosecution agreements allow companies to buy their way out of a criminal conviction."

Mr. Deaver then said, "As time has progressed, we have been working on ways to include guilty pleas and to impose felony as well as misdemeanor charges to make compliance more certain.

"Though it may appear counter-intuitive, it is overall better from a societal standpoint to develop ways to extract the correction of violations and fines but allow companies to stay in business. However, we will use the specter of a criminal conviction to achieve our goals, if that becomes necessary."

Mr. Deaver continued, "It is my intent here to form a CalEPA task force made up of the six of us to investigate environmental crimes and to utilize the various enforcement techniques available.

"We will seek to craft agreements with teeth to dissuade corporations from violating environmental laws to the detriment of the people of the State.

"We will be looking for ways to prosecute the senior executives rather than the unwitting managers, who were just carrying out orders given to them by their bosses."

Mr. Deaver was finished with his talk. It appeared as if he may have been successful in convincing the other four people on the task force that he intended to aggressively pursue corporations for environmental law violations, including using criminal sanctions and prosecuting those in upper management.

Taylor, however, was not convinced. She was getting that sinking feeling that when push came to shove, she would be the only person who would be willing to bring the full weight of the Attorney General's Office against the perpetrators. Her sense was that this task force might be nothing more than business as usual.

Mr. Deaver excused the group. Taylor returned her rental car, was given a ride back to her hotel, packed, and flew home to her waiting husband.

Chapter Three
The Story of Me

We have seen my introduction into the world of the environmental task force for the Office of the Attorney General of the State of California. Allow me to share my personal development.

As a pre-teen and teenager, my first exposure to men was with the men that my mother "entertained." As my mother was an alcoholic, she and her friends would invariably become fall down drunk. As her friends lost interest in her, they turned their attention to me.

I was petrified. I was so young that I did not know how to fend off their advances, and I was certainly not going to learn this from my mother.

I grew up in Newton, a poor farming community in the California desert. The closest larger town was Haven. We were not terribly far from Bryan or the Coachella Valley.

Though Newton was a farming community, farms are generally home to decent people and to women who understand hard work and strong morals, as, on a farm, women work equally hard with the men to keep the operation going.

When I was little, when my mother's friends made their advances, I was able to escape to one or two of our neighbors who allowed me to hide on their property, usually in the crawl space under the house.

When I turned 14, I began maturing into what some perverted types might think was a sexual object. While at our house, one of my mother's most awful and belligerent friends told her that he was getting tired of her, and he began coming after me. I locked myself in the bathroom. When my mother tried to intercede, he beat her, pushed her aside, and broke down the bathroom door. Fortunately, I had already escaped through the bathroom window.

This sent him into a rage. He pushed past my mother and ran out of the front door. He threatened to beat her if she did not tell him where I was going. Figuring that he would not bother to chase after me, my mother told him that I was going to my Aunt Nettie's which was about a mile away by road but only a quarter of a mile away through the woods. As it was pouring down rain with lightning and thunder, he set out after me in his truck.

Because the path through the woods was much shorter than the road, I arrived at Nettie's first.

I was hysterical. I told Nettie what had happened and that he might come here. She told me to go inside to the kitchen and call the sheriff. Knowing better than to question her, I went into the kitchen and did as she asked.

Unknown to me, Nettie took her 870 Remington shot gun out of a cabinet and loaded it.

A couple of minutes later, a very large jacked up pickup truck with multiple front head-lights pulled onto the property. The lights were pointed at the front porch and door. The guy, whose name was Ben, got out of the truck and started walking towards the front steps.

Nettie went out through the front door and stood on the porch in Ben's path. When Ben got onto her property, about 15 feet from the front steps, he said, "Where's the girl. I've come to take her."

Nettie, raised her shotgun and replied, "You will not be taking the girl from this property. Now turn around, get back in your truck, and get out of here."

Ben replied, "Not without the girl."

Ben continued to approach the porch. Nettie leveled the shotgun and shot him in the foot, just along the left side of his boot. I think he was startled that she would actually use the gun.

Nettie said, "The next one is going between your eyes."

Just then the sheriff showed up. He came over to the front yard where Ben was examining his foot. The sheriff asked, "What is going on here?"

Nettie answered, "This fellow slapped around Taylor's mother and has now chased Taylor over here. She is only 14."

Ben retorted, "She's crazy. She shot me. I want her arrested."

The sheriff calmly said, "Mister, you are very lucky that I showed up when I did. Nettie here can shoot a fly off an orange at 100 paces. The next shot would have been center mass or between your eyes, and we would be calling the coroner.

"I am going to give you 3 minutes to get out of here. If you ever so much as look at Mrs. Shaw or Taylor again, you will be going to jail for a very long time. That is, if you make it to jail. Around these parts, people do not take kindly to grown men attempting to have their way with children. Now get."

He left, and we never heard from him again. After that, my mother limited her activities in the house. She would go to the local bar if she needed to drink or whatever. It wasn't a perfect arrangement, but it was much better than before.

At 16, I met Frank Diaz. He worked on his parents' orange farm. We met while we were both delivering oranges to the central market for shipment out of the area.

He was such a nice boy. He was 18 and was planning to leave Newton and move to Haven to join the Haven-Newton Police Department. We spent hours talking about his plans. As I was only 16, my future plans had not yet been formulated.

Frank and I did not have a physical relationship. I was only 16, and in California if one is underage, it is statutory rape, regardless of whether the relationship is consensual or not. There are no defenses. Fortunately for both of us, Frank moved to Haven to start his police training before we could do anything stupid.

During this time, I was babysitting for a little girl by the name of Tammy Fitzgerald. According to my mother, Tammy's father, Don Fitzgerald, had been a star football player in high school. In his final season, it was presumed that Don would one day be playing pro football. During his football days, he met and fell in love with Diane Williams, the head cheerleader.

Diane became pregnant with a son, Jason, Tammy's older brother. In Don's final high school game, he was injured, and his football career was over. Even though Don had no pro football prospects, he and Diane married and had their child.

Don tried college, but it was not for him. As a new husband and father, he needed to make money so he became a real estate salesperson.

As he could not make enough money from sales commissions alone, he decided to buy and sell real estate, where more money could be made. This brought him in contact with Antony Carbone, a gangster who had moved to the area to retire.

Don allowed Carbone to assist him in his new real estate venture, which required breaking a few laws.

For added pressure, Don and Diane had a second child, Tammy, to add to their family.

Carbone's end game was to build a hotel and casino at the south entrance to the national park in Newton. At this time, the south entrance was rarely used because the road between Haven and Newton, the town in which the south entrance was located, was a dangerous mountain road.

Carbone tried to get the building permits necessary to build a new road from Haven to Newton which would provide access to the south entrance to the park.

Because of Carbone's reputation as a gangster, his application for a permit was turned down.

Further, to get a building permit for the road, it would be necessary to show that it would serve a community need, not just the need of Mr. Carbone.

Carbone met with the police commissioner. They decided that what Carbone needed was a local face to secure the needed permits. The police commissioner told Carbone that he had the perfect patsy, Don Fitzgerald. Carbone and Don met.

Carbone made a deal with Don that if Don would become his local face and secure the building permit for a better road, the building permit for a residential subdivision to supply a community need, and the necessary permission for his casino project, he would give Don the largest house in the new subdivision, which would be worth well over a million dollars, and he would lend his credit to Don's real estate business.

The casino project would require permission from the Department of the Interior and partnering with an Indian tribe, as only Indian tribes could conduct gambling operations in California.

Don was so desperate to have the accoutrements of money that he agreed to Carbone's terms.

To even his own amazement, Don succeeded in building both the new road and the new subdivision. He and his family moved into the new home even before the subdivision was complete.

However, he was unsuccessful in obtaining the necessary permission for the casino project, as dealing with the Department of the Interior and finding a willing Indian tribe were beyond Don's capabilities.

Carbone was mad, particularly since Don was already taking advantage of his new house.

Enraged, Carbone had Don's daughter, Tammy, kidnapped in order to persuade Don to complete his promise to deliver the casino.

A real prince.

Unknown to everyone, Tammy was hidden at Carbone's compound high in the hills above Haven.

Frank graduated from the academy just after Tammy was kidnapped. Though he was technically working for the police, he was told that this particular case was off limits to him.

He was told that he was too new to the department for such a complex case. Later it was learned that the actual reason for his exclusion was that the police department was complicit in the kidnapping, with the upper brass accepting bribes and other favors from Antony Carbone, the kidnapper.

As no ransom demand was made and no body was found, the case went cold. The case was declared closed, and a funeral was held for the child.

Not believing that Tammy was actually dead, over the next months, I mounted as much of an investigation as I could as a teenager with no family background and no connections. Anything I had to add was summarily ignored, and I was treated dismissively, as expected.

By fall, not knowing what else to do, I enrolled in school at Newton Junior College. One of my classes was Constitution 101. Our teacher introduced himself as Professor Richard Miller. He was young. He was only 29. I was 19. All of the girls were scoping him out, trying to get his attention. I have to confess that even I thought he was pretty cute, and I didn't even like guys at the time, as they were all so boring and full of themselves.

After introducing himself, he told us that he was an attorney and worked in the District Attorney's Office in Haven where he prosecuted criminals and managed criminal investigations.

It seemed to me as if he would be the perfect guy to help me with the Tammy Fitzgerald case, as I had all but given up. He was young, energetic, and idealistic. When he spoke about the Constitution, he seemed to be someone who would not just accept the conventional wisdom without questioning it.

Little did I know at the time that my first impression about him would turn out to be so right.

Was I bold or did I just feel as if I had nothing left to lose? I asked him to meet me away from campus. He finally relented and said he would.

Because I did not want anyone, particularly the other students, to know that we were meeting, I arranged for us to meet at night at a bar away from campus and not frequented by students. The bar was a country western/biker bar, where my biker friends hung out.

When Rick and I met at the bar for the first time, I explained the case to him. I particularly liked the way he listened to me and did not waste my time by trying to hit on me.

Of course, I could not see what was actually going on in his mind. Maybe he was not interested in me at all but was only interested in my case. Maybe he was actually crazy about me but was smart enough to know that my interest was in the case and that hitting on me would be counter-productive.

We sent in a drone to look at the compound. We did DNA testing. We did all of the typical investigative tricks. From the drone photos, it appeared possible that someone could be held at Carbone's compound.

When all else failed, I, being stupid, decided to hike up to the compound to have a look for myself. Rick opposed my plan but went with me anyway. I was able to get through a small break in the electric fence. I sent Rick to find my friend Moose, an ex-army Ranger, for help.

At the compound, after a fight, I was also captured. This gave me an opportunity to meet and converse with Carbone. What a tool.

In short order, Moose and his friends pulled off a daring rescue of me and Tammy, and held off all of Carbone's guards and strike force.

We returned Tammy to her mother and father. When we let Tammy out of Rick's car, Rick let down his guard a little when speaking with Tammy's mother he said that some of his interest was romantic.

He hid his romantic interest well enough throughout our ordeal that it did not interfere with our business, and for that, I was eternally grateful. Hidden or not, I cannot ask for much more.

Eventually, I came to believe that he did like me romantically right from the start. My feelings were a little more complex. Firstly, I was very young and inexperienced. I never had a real boyfriend. I did kiss him in the parking lot after finals saying that since I was no longer his student that we could go on a date, if he wished. Nothing really materialized from that.

We did have sex when we went away for the night to visit the lead detective in Tammy's kidnapping case. I think that is when my feelings really started to change.

Prior to the time with Rick, sex for me came in only one flavor: a painful combination of rough, fast, and selfish. The type of men to whom I was exposed were only interested in sex for themselves and not for their partner.

Rick, on the other hand, came to me for sex as a gentle, lengthy, and mutually gratifying human connection designed to satisfy both parties and to bring them closer together. What a concept. I learned quickly that Rick's way was the way I wanted all of my sexual encounter to be. He was my first and only, and I must say he has really spoiled me.

After our first encounter we did not have sex again for quite a long time, well after rescuing Tammy, after the court cases which brought Dan and Carbone to justice, and after college and law school. Rick was a pillar patience. He must have really loved me.

When I was young and suffered from such a horrible childhood, I often opined whether I would ever be able to love at all. I had always heard that to love someone else, you had to first learn to love yourself.

With the way that he showed me that he was interested in my life, in Tammy's case, in my case, in my education, and in my work, he taught me that I was worthy of love, and this ultimately made it possible for me to love him too.

After the cases were done and my career was underway, thankfully, Rick called. He asked to see me. I jumped at the chance. We met several times. We shared stories. We talked. We laughed. We enjoyed each other. Finally, enough trust was built that we could become lovers. And it was better than wonderful.

Finally, we met for a fancy dinner. I was dressed to the nines. I came across the crowded restaurant towards Rick and could feel the stares. I sat. Rick stood and came over next to my chair. I didn't know what he was doing. He kneeled down on one knee and proposed while showing me the beautiful diamond ring he bought for me. It took me a long time to respond, not because I had second thoughts but because I could not fully grasp what was going on. Was this man actually asking me to marry him? When I finally got a handle on what was happening, I immediately replied - "Yes."

And our most beautiful life together began.

Chapter Four
Marriage

Our wedding day was coming. We booked a reception hall at a very nice hotel. (Remember, we had already known one another for seven years.)

I fussed with a wedding dress. Rick bought a tux working on the theory that he might need one in the future.

We made up a guest list which included around 50 people total. Both of Rick's parents had past. My parents were both still alive. I felt obligated to invite my mother. Though she had almost nothing to do with my life other than to expose me to her alcoholism and poor taste in men, she was legitimately excited for me, if not more than a little jealous.

My real father, if you can call him that, found out about the upcoming event. I was told that he would be attending, invited or not. He was a real class act. At this point, Rick was in too deep to back out because of my family. We had nothing to do with them over the past several years, and it was unlikely that we would have anything to do with them in the future.

When I was young, I was introduced to Moose and Carol as someone who could help them out with an income tax audit. Their accountant failed to declare as much income as they had put in the bank. By the time that I recalculated their income and found all of the legitimate expenses their accountant failed to claim, their taxable income was pretty close to the taxable income declared on their return. They paid a little tax and a modest penalty and were good to go.

Moose was the president of the local chapter of the Motorcycle Enthusiasts of America (MEA) and ran a mail order business from which one could buy coffee mugs, tee shirts, etc. with the MEA logo.

I was enlisted to help him with his books. He introduced me to other members of the association. I did book-keeping and simple tax returns for them also.

My involvement over the years with Moose and the MEA saved my life, and I mean that literally.

As we know, when I was younger, the little girl for whom I was babysitting, Tammy Fitzgerald, was kidnapped and held at the compound of Antony Carbone. When Rick and I hiked up to the compound, I went in, and Rick went for help.

Many of the skills that I learned from Moose and his boys, all of whom were ex-Rangers and Seals, while camping and otherwise were the skills which allowed me to stay alive during my captivity.

Fortunately, Rick was able to round up Moose and his crew who extricated me and Tammy from the compound in a most active gun battle.

All through college and law school and even after I started working for the AG, I remained in touch with Moose and the crew to help with book-keeping, taxes, and, frankly, anything else needed. I owed them my life, which I mean in the most literal sense of the word.

Our wedding day came. The plan was that the actual wedding would take place outside in the courtyard of the fanciest hotel in the area, a Four Seasons. It was quite beautiful. It was surrounded by rock-scape with beautiful flowers in the earthen areas. The courtyard itself had a concrete pad for, I presume, a small band or a couple of tables.

Chairs would be neatly aligned facing the stage with a large center isle to accommodate the procession.

After the ceremony, which would be short, we would all adjourn to the reception room. There would be a sit-down dinner, desert table, and a bar. There was a small band for the obligatory first dance and then some general dancing.

The ceremony went off without a hitch. Everyone adjourned to the reception hall. Dinner was served. Deserts were eaten. And alcohol was consumed in modest amounts. I placed my mother on her best behavior in that connection. The last thing I needed on my wedding day was for people I knew to see my mother drunk.

Rick and I had our first dance. He looked so handsome in a tux. He said that I was the most beautiful person he had ever seen. But I already knew he felt that way. Anyway, love is about what you do and not what you say.

Our plan was to go around the room and speak with each person or small groups of people separately.

We spoke to Moose and Carol. Both Rick and I thanked them profusely for coming and for everything that they had done for us. They were equally gracious.

We spoke to my mother. She went on and on about the dress. Clothes are not really a big deal to me. I whispered how appreciative I was that she was on her best behavior. If you are counting, I had only about 45 minutes to an hour left to endure.

We spoke with two couples from the office. They congratulated me on landing the job with the State Attorney General. One of the men, Frank Robinson, took me aside and asked in what division I would be working. I told him that I would be working in elder abuse. I was really not at liberty to share my environmental crime duties, even with others from my office, at this time.

Bart was there. He was the one who taught me hand to hand combat on the camping trip with Moose and his friends. More importantly, he was the one who physically broke into the Carbone compound to rescue first me and then Tammy. He was not prosperous, but he cleaned up well and looked good.

It's sad that people such as Bart who have encountered untold danger and life-threatening situations to help the unprotected and to keep our country safe wind up with very little after their service is done while spoiled brats such as I who had the opportunity to get an education wind up with a great job and outward success.

Bart and I spoke for a while. Rick was quite okay with it. He had similar respect for Bart as he too had seen him in action, first hand, and boy that was really something.

Finally, an unattached man came over to us. He asked Rick if he could speak to me alone. Rick relented.

We went to the least crowded side of the room. He said to me, "Hi. I'm your father."

I recoiled. I had not seen him since I was 10 years old. He was a good-looking man in his middle fifties. My mother, though now a mess, must have been pretty attractive in her 20s. The man looked prosperous. He had on a nice dress suit and looked appropriately attired for a wedding.

I said, "What do I call you?"

He replied, "Well my name is Jerry, but you already know that. You could call me dad."

I was a little more-brisk than even I expected I might be when I said, "Let's leave it at Jerry. When you've had no communication with someone for 16 years, dad seems like a stretch."

"I'm sorry about that, but times were rough, and your mother was dragging me down."

Less than diplomatically I replied, "If times were rough for you when you were in your 30s, think about what they were like for me at 10. I had to deal with her and her drunk friends for the next several years, with no help from you. You should be ashamed of yourself leaving a 10-year old in that house. I could have been raped or worse, killed."

"I'm sorry. I didn't know it was that bad."

To that, I could only reply: "No. It was worse."

He said sheepishly, "Is there anything I can do. Do you need anything?"

I replied, "Sorry, but that ship has sailed. There is nothing that I want from you. When the going got tough, you cut out. I've found a man who would walk over hot coals for me. A man who is always there for me. A man who loves me and supports me. That is the man I want. What I want from you is to leave me alone."

He said, "I'll leave then. Sorry again."

I let him go. On one level, I felt a little bad about being so hard on him. But he is the one who made our relationship what it is – nothing.

I rejoined Rick.

Rick asked, "How did it go with your dad? It looked a little serious."

Not exactly telling the whole truth, I said, "Oh, no worries. He had to leave." (Boy am I a bad actress. I hope I never have to quit my day job.)

I was not exactly truthful with Rick which was something I hated, but I seemed to be doing it a little more lately.

We finished our rounds and headed upstairs to the honey-moon suite. We would stay the night and take off for two weeks in Hawaii the next day. I presume the guests finally went home. Now that was a night to remember. I mean the honey-moon suite part. The rest I could have lived without.

Chapter Five
Honeymoon

When his mother passed away, Rick sold their family farm. Rick had no interest in farming, in living in Newton, or in being a landlord.

He used most of the money for the down payment on our new house outside of Haven. The house was truly beautiful. 3,000 square feet with four bedrooms, four bathrooms, a large eat-in kitchen and family room combination, and a laundry room. The master bedroom was quite large with two large walk-in closets and an attached bathroom. The bathroom had a toilet, a bidet, a two-basin assembly, a spa tub, and a large stall shower with a steam nozzle.

The bathroom alone was almost as large as the farm house in which I grew up.

With the left-over money Rick purchased two first class tickets and a beautiful Airbnb house in a place called Kahala, which is outside of Waikiki towards Diamond.

We left in the morning of the day after our wedding and, and with the time difference, we arrived at the Honolulu airport mid-day.

When one arrives in Honolulu, he or she is struck by the beauty of the landscape and the light, moist wind. Nothing like the desert. It is so incredible.

Rick went across the street to rent a car. I stayed at the airport with the bags. Rick entered the airport, picked up me and the luggage, and off we went. We entered the freeway heading towards Diamond Head.

The freeway runs just inland. We exited the freeway and turned left on Ala Moana Boulevard. We then turned on Kalakaua Avenue, which is the main street running through downtown Waikiki. At the end of Waikiki, we passed the park, entered Diamond Head Road, and turned onto Kahala Avenue.

We found the house. It was beautiful. It looked more similar to something one might see on the mainland with high gabled roof lines. It had a private pool and was just steps to a private beach.

If one were looking for a tropical paradise, this would be it.

We parked the car and dragged our luggage in through the front door. The house was very large. They say it sleeps 10 people. But there would only be the two of us for the next two weeks.

We changed clothes and met up on the couch in the family room. It looked over the yard and down to the ocean. It was spectacular.

Rick and I had spent the last 10 years working. We first had to prove to ourselves that Tammy, my babysitting charge, was still alive. We then had to find her at the gangster's compound.

We then had to confirm that she was actually there. In the process of doing this, I was captured and held. Then Moose and his gang had to rescue us.

After returning Tammy to her parents, we spent the next several years unraveling the kidnapping and confinement issues both criminally and civilly.

During this time, I was in school more than full time graduating from college and law school by the time I was 25 and beginning to work at the State Attorney General's Office full time. Rick remained with the DA all of this time, rising to the level of senior trial deputy.

Though it was rewarding watching Tammy's father and the gangster Antony Carbone lose all of their property, including their houses, and their freedom, and collecting enough in civil damages to finance law school, it was a long and arduous process complicated by the fact that I was in school full time, and Rick was working.

I found an outside contractor to manage the farm for my mother. He was able to make enough on the orange crop to pay the mortgage, my mother's modest living expenses, and to give her a small allowance. I would not have been able to take on law school if I had to continue as my mother's caretaker.

After all of this, when Rick wanted to rekindle our relationship after I started working, it was hard. But we managed. I guess after all that Rick went through for me, even I, one of the most damaged people I knew, was able to finally learn to trust him. Talk about making things difficult.

We dated, became lovers, got engaged, and got married. As Rick had predicted, I was elevated at the AG's office. This was good and bad. It was good because it was what I wanted from a career standpoint. It was bad because my increased responsibilities and travel would eventually affect our relationship.

My new position was, by its nature, very secretive. I would be investigating and prosecuting environmental crimes committed by people very high up in major corporations who would be trying their hardest to deny liability and to blame the rank and file working people for their crimes.

Ultimately, it would be me against corporate CEOs. There has been nothing like it since David took on Goliath, and David did not have their kind of money or resources, if you follow me.

But for the next two weeks, we put everything aside. We forgot how we got here and just remembered that we were here and in love.

I was wearing a wrap over a two-piece bathing suit. Rick was wearing a tee shirt and bathing suit. We walked across the yard and onto our private beach. The water was very warm, around 80 degrees. It felt so good. Rick remarked how well I filled out the small bathing suit I was wearing. He looked pretty good himself. He was an exercise nut and did weights several times a week.

After a swim, we came back, and jumped in the pool. The pool's water was colder than the ocean.

The nice thing about having a house is that we could cook. We didn't have to go out for every meal.

We made dinner. Rick broiled a couple of small steaks which we had with pasta and a salad. We were both starved.

After dinner, we cleaned up the kitchen and retired to the bedroom. The bedroom would see much action over the next two weeks. We finally had a chance to really hit our stride as lovemakers. I think we are both pretty good at it, but we loved each other so much and on so many levels that it would be pretty hard to miss.

The next day, we caught a bus to Hanauma Bay. It is located on the southeast coast of Oahu, not far from our house. It is known for snorkeling. We put on our gear and snorkeled for a couple of hours. The bay is so calm and the fish are so tame it's as if one is swimming in a tropical fish tank.

The bus let us off in Waikiki so we walked to an early dinner upstairs at Chuck's Steak House. The food was great. We made our way home.

The next day we relaxed. We had a dinner cruise planned. Though it sounds a little corny, it was fun.

The next day was a luau, which was also fun.

We had a rental car so the next day we headed off to the north shore. We drove back towards the airport, turned by the University, and drove through the island. As the north shore loomed in the distance, pineapple fields surrounded the highway.

When the highway reaches the north shore, it bends to the right and runs along the shoreline of several famous surfing beaches. There is Haleiwa, Waimea Bay, Banzai Pipeline, and Sunset Beach, to name a few. It was not winter, and none of the beaches were breaking to any extent.

We returned back through Waikiki. We stopped and had dinner at Duke's, which is literally in the center of town and very crowded.

We returned to our house where we stayed until the next day. For the next couple of days, we hung out at the house, by the pool and in the ocean. Rick tried his hand at surfing, which he says he did as a kid. He was still pretty good.

For the next week, we relaxed and did a few tourist-like activities including the Pearl Harbor tour, a trip around the east side of the island past Sandy Beach to Kailua. We returned through the tunnel to Honolulu and then back to our house.

Towards the end of our trip, we ventured to the west side to see Makaha, which, according to Rick, is a famous surfing beach.

Unfortunately, our trip was drawing to a close. On Sunday, we packed up and flew back to Los Angeles, from where we arranged transportation for the three-hour trip to our home in the desert.

We arrived home completely trashed. Neither of us was looking forward to returning to work on Monday.

Chapter Six
Taylor's Return to the Attorney General's Office

According to the California Constitution, the duty of the office of the California Attorney General is to ensure that "the laws of the state are uniformly and adequately enforced."

This work is done through the California Department of Justice, which employs over 1,100 attorneys.

The California AG is elected for a four-year term, with a maximum of two terms.

Originally, the AG lacked jurisdiction over matters within the jurisdiction of the local district attorneys and sheriffs. That was changed in 1934.

Presently, the State Attorney General is the State's chief law officer, heads the State Department of Justice, acts as chief counsel in State litigation, and oversees law enforcement agencies, including the local district attorneys and sheriffs.

The AG's duties include:
1. Providing consumer protection from fraud, scams, and dangerous products;
2. Protecting the state's natural resources by upholding state and federal environmental laws;
3. Providing oversight or becoming directly involved in criminal court cases and appeals;
4. Assisting in the enforcement of judgments for such things a child support, victim's programs, elder abuse, tax evasion, and intellectual property theft; and
5. Generally protecting the rights and interests of the people of the state.

The AG's office also has an administrative component. Complaints are acted upon only after there is a comprehensive investigation by the AG's investigators and a deputy AG. If warranted, the case is assigned to a different deputy AG for further action.

I was initially drawn to the AG's office because I felt that its mission was more to utilize the law to protect the interests of the people rather than merely for punishment, extracting fines, and obtaining money damages from large corporations.

My initial work was in elder abuse. I thought we did great work helping the elderly with access, housing, and other services. As Rick predicted, I would soon be promoted to white collar crimes, as it was the most complicated (and visible) work done by our office.

Much of the white-collar crime centers around environmental issues. To take the short cuts necessary to make more money, a major corporation might dispose of its toxic waste in a way that damages the environment. As a consequence, intended or otherwise, the lives of the people and wildlife living in that environment would be affected adversely, often in very serious ways.

Our office fights this. One thing we did recently was to establish the Bureau of Environmental Justice.

We also work with the federal EPA to help them with environmental crimes taking place in our State.

As I mentioned before, one reason that I was chosen to be part of the environmental task force under the leadership of Mr. Deaver is that it was thought that my geographic area, which has little industry, would leave me free to travel to other locations to partner with one of our other task force members to help with environmental enforcement issues in his location.

Mr. Deaver advised me that this might entail some traveling. He said that he knew that I was a newlywed. I told him that though technically a newlywed, my husband and I had been together, one way or another, for nearly 10 years. Some trips for business would be expected. Also, my husband was asked to return to Newton Junior College to give some guest lectures, which would keep him pretty busy too.

I worked on several interesting cases.

One case involved a furniture operation. The operator sprayed methyl chloride onto the furniture to strip it and allowed the drippings to flow into a floor drain, which is connected to the sewer.

Methyl chloride is classified as hazardous waste which must be disposed of at a permitted hazardous waste disposal facility, and the sewer is not such a facility. Our office brought a criminal action in coordination with the local District Attorney's Office.

Another case was one involving the BC Stocking Distributing Corp., a wholesaler and retailer of fuel. The company was permitted by the State to store up to 20,000 gallons of used oil in two above-ground tanks. However, state inspectors found that the company was storing more than the allotted amount, a clear violation of law.

I found it interesting to note that some hospital waste is considered toxic waste. The ordinary waste can be disposed of without special handling. But the toxic waste portion must be disposed of by legal means.

I got involved with the AG to help people. But I must confess that the more I learn about white collar crime the less good I feel about what we are doing about it.

When companies are allowed to utilize deferred and non-prosecution agreements they are essentially being allowed to buy their way out of a criminal conviction.

Rather than pleading guilty to a crime, they agree to pay fines. This allows the company to escape the stigma of a criminal conviction.

The prosecution often opines that by entering into a non-prosecution agreement, the company's board will assist the government in pursuing criminal charges against executives.

In a case involving Monsanto, prosecutors were blocked from charging the company with a felony for illegal spraying of pesticides in Hawaii and were instructed to reduce the charges to a misdemeanor. A deferred prosecution agreement did extract a 10 million dollar fine but will allow the charges to be dismissed if the company abides by its compliance plan.

An interesting question to ponder is this: With a white-collar crime, do wealthy professionals inflict more or less harm than your run-of-the mill minor criminal inflicts when committing a street crime?

It has been shown that white collar crime may cost its victims $300 to $800 billion per year while street crimes such as burglary, larceny, etc. cost victims around $16 billion.

Street crimes committed by lower class criminals are handled by policemen, prosecutors, and judges where penalties include fines, imprisonment, etc. With white collar crime, there is often no official action or arrest at all, just suits for damages in civil court, the invitation to an administrative hearing, or a fine.

Regardless of the mission of anyone else in the AG's office, my personal mission is to hold the corporate officers who order the commission of the acts accountable to the full extent of the law rather than allowing them to sacrifice their managers or employees.

Believe it or not, I was actually given an assistant. She is a brand-new attorney. Her name is Amanda Warren. She was given to me primarily to do research, something for which I had little time. However, I thought to myself that teaching her how to do research might take more time than just doing the research myself.

I came to learn that this was not the case at all. Not only was she smart with the makings of a good attorney, she ultimately became the first close personal female friend that I would ever have.

The Trump Administration promoted several changes in the environmental law. His theory appeared to be that if we loosen environmental regulations, businesses will be able to redirect the money necessary for compliance to greater production and profit.

Provided that the sidestepping of certain regulations does not endanger people or the environment, this may be a plausible approach.

Amanda's first research assignment was to assemble some of the changes made or proposed by the Trump Administration. They included the following.

1. Pulling out of the Paris Climate Agreement
2. Scraping the Clean Power Plant plan.
3. Loosening regulations on toxic air pollution.
4. Rescinding methane-flaring rules
5. Weakening the Obama era fuel economy rules.
6. Revoking the Obama era requirement that rising sea levels be factored into federally funded construction projects.
7. Narrowing the definition of what is considered federally protected waters.
8. Allowing the use of seismic air-gun blasts for oil and gas drilling.
9. Easing restrictions against mining and drilling in the habitat of the sage grouse.
10. Proposing changes to the Endangered Species Act.

11. Recognizing that companies installing wind turbines will no longer be in violation of the Migratory Bird Treaty Act if their activities kill birds.
12. Opening public lands for mining and drilling.
13. Increasing logging on public lands.
14. Dropping climate change from the list of national security threats.
15. Investigating why the EPA's criminal enforcement is at a 30 year low.

Under the Trump Administration, the size and influence of the EPA shrunk, and there are far fewer criminal prosecutions for environmental crimes.

Amanda and I went through the various changes. With the Biden Administration it is presumed that some of the changes will be reversed.

For me personally, I prefer to use the specter of a criminal prosecution to encourage companies to follow through on their promised cleanups. Otherwise, they are able to avoid sanctions with bankruptcy and by other means.

Amanda agreed with me. I think that the two of us feel pretty much the same way about the importance of our work and will work together to best protect the public from the polluters.

While I continued on with the AG and the task force, Rick was again taking up his teaching duties at Newton JC.

Chapter Seven
Rick's First Guest Lecture

"Hello everyone. My name is Professor Richard Miller. You can call me Professor Miller, or, if you wish, you can call me Rick.

"I have been asked to give a lecture on the Constitution and its aftermath to supplement your American History class.

"After the conclusion of the French-Indian War in 1763, the British were required to assume greater responsibilities in the colonies. To pay for these responsibilities, it decided to impose various taxes and regulations on colonial trade and business activities.

"To this end, Britain enacted the Sugar Act, the Stamp Act, the Townshend Act, and other laws taxing the colonists. The colonists responded with its famous battle cry, 'No taxation without representation.'

"Sentiment began to move from opposing commercial regulations to declaring independence.

"The Boston Massacre occurred, the Boston Tea Party took place, and the First Continental Congress met. In 1775, the shot heard around the world was fired in Lexington and Concord, and the Revolutionary War was underway.

"In 1775, the Second Continental Congress met. There was not an immediate declaration of independence, but George Washington was given command of the army.

"King George III's open hostility to the colonial uprising was evidenced by a decree from Parliament closing all American ports.

"Public opinion began to shift towards independence. Thomas Paine's Common Sense was published. Thomas Jefferson's Declaration of Independence was approved on July 4, 1776.

"War raged on for seven years. The Battle of Saratoga brought France into the war on the side of the colonists, which tipped the scale in America's favor. The Treaty of Paris was signed in 1783, which provided for American independence.

"In 1777, the Articles of Confederation were adopted. Under the Articles, each State retained complete sovereignty. Under it, Congress lacked the power to tax, to pay the debts of the States, to impose duties, to regulate commerce, to control the money supply, or to wage war.

"The decision was made to adopt a new Constitution.

"At the Constitutional Convention, there were 55 founders. 40 held public securities. A public security is effectively a debt owed by the government. 14 founders were land speculators. 24 loaned money at interest. 11 had mercantile, manufacturing, and shipping interests. And 15 owned slaves. Not one member of the Convention represented the small farming or mechanical class.

"To maintain a sufficient relationship with the south to encourage it to remain in the new union, the new Constitution provided that Congress could not prohibit slavery until 1808. Also, the three-fifth rule was implemented which would allow slaves to be counted as three-fifths of a person for the purposes of representation in the lower house of Congress. This had the consequence, perhaps unintended, of giving some slave states a greater number of electoral votes than States with more eligible voters.

"As we may see, the interests of the holders of public securities, land speculators, money lenders, those with mercantile interests, and slave owners, did receive some specific protections under the new Constitution. Was it a coincidence that they were the very people who attended the Convention?

"The interests of small farmers and mechanics were not considered at the Convention, and no one from these classes was present.

"In my opinion, with which you may certainly disagree, I believe that the religious training of the founders shows itself more in the moral underpinning of their endeavor than it does in the creation of a religious document.

"Many argue that the Constitution and the Declaration of Independence should be read together as our founding documents. In this way, Christianity could be more directly infused into our laws. However, this reading fails to mention that more than a dozen years elapsed between the Declaration and the Constitution, that the documents were written for different purposes by different people, and that for the approximately dozen years between the two, the Articles of Confederation, a secular document, was the central governing document of the country.

"The Declaration states that all men are endowed by their Creator with certain unalienable rights including life, liberty, and the pursuit of happiness. However, it also states that governments derive their power from the consent of the governed, that is, from people and not from God.

"The Declaration states that when people seek the station in life to which they are entitled, they rely on the Laws of Nature and Nature's God. This God does not appear to be the Christian God but rather Nature's God, a deist concept, which stands to reason as the document was written by a deist, Thomas Jefferson.

"I believe that the Constitution is a highly moral document written by highly moral people, but I do not believe that it needs to be considered a Christian document.

"I prefer to look at the Declaration of Independence as being just that, a declaration; a letter to the King advising him of the many transgressions of which he was accused and demanding independence.

"Many revolutions have an element of redistribution of property, most notably the Russian and Cuban revolutions. Not much is said about property redistribution following the American Revolution. Perhaps this is because the American Revolution has been highly romanticized over the years, and redistribution of wealth is considered a despotic and not a romantic concept.

"During the American Revolution, many states passed laws allowing colonists to seize property belonging to loyalists.

"I do not add this to show that the revolutionaries were bad people but only to show that they were human. I personally favor looking at the events in a realistic way, as in this manner, we may better assess the founding from a standpoint of history, rather than theatre. I am most happy to entertain all schools of thought, different or not.

"This brings us to the election of George Washington as our first President. He served from roughly 1789 to 1796. Under the electoral college system, he was elected by the electors appointed from the several States. Each State received as many electoral votes as it had members of the House of Representatives and Senate.

"In those days, when they actually followed the procedure set out in Article II, the electors met and voted. In the case of George Washington, the vote was unanimous, as was expected. George Washington was inaugurated in April, 1789. John Adams received the second most votes and became Vice-President. This was changed by the 12th Amendment.

"Washington started many customs which would be followed by subsequent Presidents. One of the first of these was to appoint a cabinet. Among others, he selected Thomas Jefferson as Secretary of State and Alexander Hamilton as Secretary of the Treasury. This would be the functional equivalent of selecting LeBron James and Steph Curry for your basketball team.

"During the Washington Administration, the Judiciary Act created the circuit courts and the district courts on the federal level. The Supreme Court was created by Article III.

"The Bill of Rights was ratified on December 15, 1791. During the ratification contest for the new Constitution, five states demanded a Bill of Rights to protect the peoples' rights against the new federal government. Originally, the provisions of the Bill of Rights applied only to actions taken by the new federal government. Its protections were not applied to actions taken by the States until the 14th Amendment which was enacted after the Civil War.

"Alexander Hamilton as Secretary of the Treasury set out to implement some of the provisions of the new Constitution including paying the national debt, paying the holders of public securities (State debt), and working out a system of tariffs.

"In the 1770s, the British imposed taxes and regulations on the American colonies. Negotiations failed. A group of rich, white Americans, including George Washington, embarked upon the Revolutionary War.

"The rich, white men enlisted lower-class white men and slaves to join them in fighting. After seven long years, the Americans won the War.

"During the Revolutionary War, both the national and State governments borrowed money from foreign governments and ordinary citizens. The creditors were issued bonds or public securities. After the War, the confederation lacked the money to pay these debts.

"Under the Articles of Confederation, Congress had only the power to requisition money from the States; it had no power to tax. Most States declined to pay the money requisitioned. This meant that unless the system was changed, some debts might go unpaid.

"Many rich, white men made investments in pre-Constitution debt (public securities). 40 of the 55 founders had such investments, some of which were purchased at a discount.

"When Hamilton became Secretary of the Treasury, his plan was for the new government to repay both the national and State debts. This would make the United States a very good credit risk for countries wishing to do business with it, he reasoned.

"Congress approved full repayment of both the national and State debt. No States opposed the repayment of the national debt. However, some of the southern States opposed the repayment of the State debt, as most of the southern States had already repaid their share of that debt. A compromise was reached in which the southern States would allow the new government to repay the State debt in exchange for the US capital being located in the south.

"Hamilton asked Congress for a protective tariff to raise money and to protect local industry. The tariff passed.

"Article VI of the new Constitution provided that all debts entered into before the Constitution shall be valid against the United States after the Constitution.

"Compromises were made between the north and south. For the north, State debts were assumed by the new government, and tariffs were allowed. For the south, slavery would not be prohibited prior to 1808, and fugitive slave laws would be enforced.

"The Constitution was ratified by conventions within the States, that is, by groups of insiders chosen for the purpose of ratification, and not by the people or even by the State Legislatures. One could question whether the Constitution actually ever passed as a piece of legislation.

"As added cover, the new federal government would utilize the same restrictive voting requirements followed by the States, including property ownership in most States.

"During the Washington Administration, Alexander Hamilton, as Secretary of the Treasury, repaid the national and State debts with money generated by tariffs, without the need of an income tax. (Where is he when we need him now?)

"Rich, white men organized the war, fought the war, fixed the interim government, and established a permanent government. It's not much of a stretch to see that the end product might reflect their needs.

"But might the more interesting question be whether they left enough room for other groups to succeed within this framework? Some would argue yes; others would argue no.

"We will look at the development of the country in the 1800s. Remember, hundreds of primarily white men fought the Civil War to bring an end to slavery. The 13th, 14th, and 15th Amendments were then enacted.

"George Washington declined a third term. His stepping down signaled to the rest of the world that the American experiment was working. His Farewell Address warned against entangling alliances with other countries, which became impossible to achieve.

"This brings us to the end of Washington's administration. I will see you at our next lecture."

Chapter Eight
Taylor Arriving Home at Last

I got home from work at around 8:30, and I still beat Rick. He was lecturing at the junior college and would not be home until almost 9. I took off my heels, pulled on my sweat pants, got a glass of wine, and retired to the couch to wait for him. I watched TV for a few minutes when Rick came in through the front door.

"Hi, honey. I'm home."

When I was 17, never in my wildest dreams did I think that I would ever hear those words directed to me. Really nice.

"I'm in here."

Rick came into the TV room and sat next to me on the couch. He put my feet in his lap and began giving me a foot massage. One of the benefits of being married.

I asked, "How was your day?"

"Good. Worked and gave my lecture. It went longer than I hoped. Got through the Washington Administration. Some of the same old stuff you have heard over the years. But I think it is important."

Though I trust Rick implicitly, I asked this question as a mild joke, sort of, "Did any of your girl students linger around your desk after class to see if they could get help for an outside project from their professor?"

Rick responded, "No. I don't know anyone that bold, at least anymore."

I replied, "Ha. Ha. I was just kidding."

"I know. How was your day?"

I replied, "You know me. Looking for EPA violations from whistleblowers, web-sites, and tips, the usual stuff."

Rick and I didn't like secrets, but some of my work was pretty confidential as it involved possible criminal violations by major corporations. Also, the work was pretty boring. It was usually just easier to say things were as usual.

Rick's day job was similar in the boring department. The crimes with which he dealt were of the street crime variety, but it would still be unfair to discuss anyone's problems, regardless of their magnitude.

Rick went off to bed leaving me on the couch with the TV. This was not a bad thing. This gave me time to think about the cases being prosecuted and those becoming ripe for prosecution.

I felt that things were going well in the AG's office. Trust me, this was not because I was particularly bright or gifted but because I was willing to work hard and to be ruthless with these corporate-types, even when everyone else was pussy-footing around them, including my bosses.

As we know, Ron Patterson, a young, good looking black guy, was the head of our little office in Fairview. He was, of course, responsible for all of the work we had. My environmental work was not our primary business, but I reported to Mr. Patterson for most of my work and to Mr. Deaver in the Sacramento office for the environmental work.

Mr. Deaver and Mr. Patterson had an arrangement where if it was possible due to my case load, I could partner with another environmental lawyer and work with him or her, as there was not much industry in the desert where we were located. However, two attorneys were often needed for the larger cases in Los Angeles and San Diego.

After a couple of investigations, I was beginning to see the handwriting on the wall. Most of the AG's attorneys were just not willing to unleash the full weight of the office against CEOs.

I think that everyone involved in white collar crime knew that the AG's office was just a stepping stone. We were paid barely a living wage to take on some really complicated and time-consuming cases but knew that after a few years we could switch to the other side and represent the corporations, and make some real money. Most of our opponents were represented by the largest, most powerful law firms in the country.

It seemed as if no one was willing to be the bad guy because he was afraid that he would not get hired by the big firms after his or her stint in the AG's office was over.

I, on the other hand, did not give a rip about money or about working for a large corporate law firm. Rick and I would do fine, even if I couldn't get a cushy job.

I only knew one way to do a job, and that was all the way.

Political pressure was also being brought to bear. In Washington, the more conservative administration was pressing for more corporate latitude in the realm of environment protection. The move was for less regulation rather than more, as Amanda and I discussed at length.

The pendulum was swinging. By the early 1980s the enforcement of environmental laws was becoming tougher with criminal penalties being possible. By the second decade of the 2000s, less enforcement was being pressed.

In Sacramento, Mr. Deaver was beginning to sense the way I felt, and, frankly, I don't think he liked it.

Unknown to me, he arranged with my boss for me to fly to Sacramento to see him in his office. Mr. Patterson could not decline, even if he wanted to.

I joined Rick in bed. The next morning, we woke up and had breakfast. Rick drove to his office. I drove to mine. When I arrived, I received the news from Mr. Patterson that Mr. Deaver needed to see me in Sacramento.

My secretary, Marjorie Goodman, made my travel arrangements for later that day. (Yes, I was actually given a secretary. A subtle indication that my work at the office was actually recognized as work.) Amanda would not be making this trip.

I called Rick and told him that I had to go to Sacramento and that if I made it back, it would be late. He said okay. He was very understanding, as always.

Chapter Nine
Sacramento With Mr. Deaver

I flew out and arrived in the Sacramento office at 4 in the afternoon. I checked in with the receptionist and was asked to wait in the waiting area. Mr. Deaver came out and took me to his private office. It was one of the larger, corner offices around the perimeter of the building. I was asked to be seated.

He started: "Well, Ms. Shaw, I hear that you are really trying to shake things up down in Fairview."

I replied, "How do you mean sir?"

"I've heard that you want to go after corporate executives with felony convictions and long prison sentences?"

I calmly replied, "For some of the crimes I've seen, if deterrence is our objective, I believe that both would be necessary."

He replied, less calmly, "Isn't that a little harsh?"

I said, "I really don't think so. Let's have a look at the Port Arthur Chemical case. The President of the company admitted that he did not properly protect his employees from exposure to hydrogen sulfide, resulting in the death of two employees.

"For killing two people, he was sentenced to 12 months in prison and ordered to pay a fine of $5,000. $5,000. is a joke. They have more than that in the petty cash drawer. And we both know that of a 12-month sentence, he probably won't serve 90 days. All pretty light for killing two people. At this rate, a corporate officer cannot afford to not break the law."

Mr. Deaver added, "I thought that it was a fair result."

I could not resist, "A fair result for whom, not for the families of the two truck drivers who were killed. Who feeds those families? Who puts those kids through college?"

"What would you suggest?"

"I would suggest a little more judicial violence. The Courts are up to the task. Just look at the United States vs. Elias. Elias failed to supply his employee with safety equipment for cyanide gas poisoning, and he was sentenced to 17 years in prison, the longest sentence ever imposed for an environmental crime.

"I would suggest that we press harder than we are pressing now. Particularly if death is involved, we owe it to the people to pursue the ultimate order givers and not just the order takers."

Then, putting my foot further into my mouth, I said, "It is my personal opinion that if death results, we should pursue not only involuntary manslaughter, which does not carry much of a penalty, but also murder in the second degree, for which the penalties are much more severe."

Believe it or not, Mr. Deaver tried this with me: "Well, Ms. Shaw, you are going to have to slow down a little."

He was basically speaking to me as if I was a fourth-grader who was sent to the principal's office.

He went on, "We need to come to an understanding. I might need to take you off of the task force and let you get back to your other duties where you can't do as much damage."

I was indignant and replied, "Damage. That's rich. Going after corporate big wigs who, in pursuit of profits, allow their employees to die rather than spend a little extra money to protect them is damage?"

He retorted, "I understand that you are young and idealistic. I will take that into account when evaluating your performance. That's all I have today. I wanted to give you a heads up in person rather than over the phone. I'll take everything you said into consideration. We can talk more later. For now, I have to get home, or my wife will kill me. Have a safe flight back."

I got up and left his office. He's worried about his wife pretend-killing him for being late but does not seem concerned at all about two truck drivers who were actually killed by the greed of their boss.

They got me a cab to the airport. I flew home. I reached my house at 10 p.m.

―――

After I left, while traveling home, and clearly out of ear-shot, Mr. Deaver picked up his cell phone and called someone I did not know. I believe that this person was his boss or some business associate from a business outside of the AG's office.

He spoke into the phone, "I spoke with Ms. Shaw about your concerns. I tried to cool her off. At this point, there is nothing we can do about using criminal penalties in these prosecutions. That cat is already out of the bag. We have been using criminal penalties for so long that if we stop using them now, we will be viewed as being too soft on crime.

"But not to worry. I have spoken to all of the other task force members, and they are all on board with the idea of allowing the companies to postpone criminal prosecution so long as the fines are paid.

"Also, they appear to be okay with going after the underlings and not the upper officers, such as you, so long as they have the opportunity to receive some future consideration for their trouble, like a cushy job at one of the firms you use.

"She, of course, is not interested in making any such deals; she's such a straight arrow. She's really a pain."

Mr. Deaver waited while the person on the other end of the line said something to him.

Then Mr. Deaver spoke into the receiver again, "I'm sorry, but I had to put her on the task force. We needed a woman, and she is the only woman in the entire office who is even remotely qualified. But I will have Patterson assign her some other types of cases, to the extent that he can."

Mr. Deaver, being the coward that he is, was afraid to tell the person on the other end of the line that Taylor was talking about going after the higher-ups in the corporate organizations and in ramping up the criminal charges to include murder in the second degree, if death should occur.

Mr. Deaver arrived home. He took a little flak from his wife, which he had heard a million times before, as if he was immune.

Chapter Ten
Taylor, Rick, and Environmental Law

Taylor arrived home at 10 p.m. She slipped into bed, and she and Rick slept until morning. It was Saturday, so neither had to go to work.

They had breakfast. After breakfast, Taylor broached the subject.

"Honey, a couple of interesting things transpired over the last few days."

Rick interjected, "Don't tell me. They are going to give you a promotion and the big raise that you so richly deserve?"

"Well, not exactly."

Taylor went on to relate her conversation with Mr. Deaver. She told Rick that in connection with her environmental law duties, she was actually being dressed down for being too aggressive with the corporate higher-ups.

She told him that when she mentioned that when there was a death involved that she might seek murder two instead of involuntary manslaughter, Mr. Deaver seemed to become really agitated.

She did not generally discuss her work with Rick because she deemed it to be too sensitive. But she said that she was feeling a little threatened and thought that Rick should know about this discussion in case she needed his support or cover in the future.

Also, Rick was a real expert in criminal law, having been in the trenches of criminal prosecutions and investigations for over a dozen years.

She explained to Rick that in the early 1980s they began using criminal penalties to enforce environmental laws. This came about because previously it was deemed to be more cost effective to violate the law and pay the fines than to obey the law, particularly when liability could be shifted to a manager or low-level employee. The prospect of a criminal penalty became the only possible deterrent.

Taylor's point was that criminal penalties have been used for years, but when they were not used, the results were not good.

For example, in 2015, a case was brought against Exide Technologies in Vernon to cover the cost of decontaminating its plant and the surrounding neighborhood. Federal prosecutors did not file criminal charges against the company or its executives in what is known as a non-prosecution agreement. Eventually, the company went bankrupt and did not pay the full cost of the cleanup.

All of the illegal dumping that occurred contaminated the ground water, plants, and animals which ultimately injures people. Unfortunately, the time between the dumping and the injury is so remote that it is nearly impossible to prove a connection between the two.

Taylor said that in her lifetime, we may make some strides to correct these wrongs, but it will be difficult. Taylor went on to say that within her present capabilities, her disagreement with Mr. Deaver was really over cases where death occurs almost immediately after the illegal act so that causation is obvious.

She went back to the classic case of Port Arthur Chemical that she discussed with Mr. Deaver in Sacramento.

In that case, the company had its employees transport waste water containing hydrogen sulfide. Not only did they falsify documents to conceal the fact that the waste water came from Port Arthur, but they failed to properly protect their employees. Two employees died as a result.

A guilty plea was accepted for an OSHA violation. The sentence imposed was 12 months in federal prison and a fine of $5,000., for two deaths. Taylor thought that this sentence was a complete joke.

She said that her difference with Mr. Deaver was not so much that the fine was too small, but, more importantly, that she thought that the employer should have been charged with second degree murder rather than involuntary manslaughter.

Taylor and Rick discussed the difficulty of charging a company with manslaughter. Under the common law, a company could be prosecuted for manslaughter only if a member of the company was prosecuted and only if that member was the "controlling mind" of the company.

In small companies it was not difficult to find a person who was the controlling mind. However, in large companies, there often would not be a single person who was the "controlling mind," and even if there was, he might not be personally liable for the death if the death was caused by someone else.

Taylor stated that because of this, the common law was replaced by statutes which made the imposition of a such a sentence more possible.

Rick made some interesting points about murder and manslaughter generally. He said that in order of severity, there is first degree murder, second degree murder, voluntary manslaughter, and involuntary manslaughter.

First degree murder is generally reserved for premeditated homicides. Voluntary manslaughter is generally for heat of passion killings.

Involuntary manslaughter generally requires a killing in the commission of a non-dangerous misdemeanor or criminal negligence.

Second degree murder generally requires malice aforethought but such malice may be implied when one acts with an abandoned and malignant heart, with conscious disregard for life, or during the commission of a non-listed felony.

Rick said that the line between second degree murder and involuntary manslaughter is finer than one might think. However, the distinction becomes very important when it comes to sentencing. Involuntary manslaughter carries a prison sentence of up to 4 years, while second degree murder carries a prison sentence of 15 years to life. Rick stated the obvious. The difference is significant.

Rick said that in his cases he presses for second degree murder where there is a conscious disregard for life. If we look at the Port Arthur case, we see that the defendant admitted that he did not properly protect his employees from exposure to a poisonous gas which he knew could cause serious injury or death.

He then posed the question: Isn't that a conscious disregard of life?

Taylor told Rick that in 2019, the Trump Administration's Justice Department intervened to block prosecutors from charging Monsanto with a felony for illegally spraying a toxic pesticide in Hawaii. The charges were reduced to misdemeanors.

Monsanto pleaded guilty to the misdemeanor charges, and prosecutors used a deferred prosecution agreement to extract a 10 million dollar fine. If the company sticks to its compliance plan, the felony charges will be dismissed.

Taylor told Rick that according to what she has read, there has been a dramatic decrease in environmental crime prosecutions.

After their long talk, Taylor thought to herself how lucky she was to have a husband who was not only good to her but who was also a good listener.

Rick said, "Well, it sounds as if you have your work cut out for you with this gang. If I didn't know better, I would not be surprised to learn that their end game was something other than enforcing our State's environmental laws."

"I can't disagree with you," was all Taylor would say.

Chapter Eleven
Taylor on Girlfriends

"I've personally have never had much interest in girlfriends."

Taylor delivered this pronouncement while seated at a table in the bar located on the ground floor of her office building. She was speaking with Amanda Warren, the newest hire at the AG's office. Amanda had just come on board. They were both nursing screw drivers after a long day at the office.

Though she was not familiar with Amanda's background or work experience, she did think that she may have been brought in to have a second woman attorney in the office. She did learn that Amanda went to law school at Stanford, certainly one of the best in the nation, and had no previous work experience, which was not unusual for the type of job she was doing.

Amanda was young, around 25, and pretty enough, which never hurts when applying for a job. She was dressed appropriately in a grey business suit, blouse, skirt to the knees, nylons, and low heels. Very similar to the way Taylor was dressed, except that Taylor's suit was navy blue.

Amanda asked, "Why would you say that?"

"Seems as if every time I try to strike up a relationship with another woman, particularly a young woman, they become competitive, and things disintegrate from there. I have never been able to understand why minorities, and I refer to a woman working in a white man's world as a minority, cannot stick together and support one another. Instead, they try to advance themselves at the expense of their co-workers, including other women."

Amanda then said, "I have learned from years of undergraduate school and law school that what you say is probably true. All of my so-called girlfriends wound up being competitive with me, even if I tried to not engender those feelings."

Taylor responded, "It is really too bad. I think that as a group, we could get much more accomplished by working together.

"My best luck has been with older women. I had a great relationship with my friend's wife, but as I think back on it, I put in a great deal of work to make her feel needed, and I was teaching her things that were beneficial to both her and her husband."

Amanda asked, "What was that?"

Taylor replied, "I was teaching her how to help her husband run his business, something which they both sorely needed."

Taylor then changed the subject and said, "You are really a beautiful girl. Do you have a husband or serious boyfriend?"

"No. Neither. But thank you for the compliment. As busy as I have been, I have not had a chance to establish anything with anyone. How about you?"

"I'm married."

Amanda said, "That stands to reason. A beautiful, intelligent woman with a job. Is 'Shaw' your husband's last name or your maiden name?"

Taylor replied, "No, 'Shaw' is my maiden name. My husband's last name is 'Miller.' We decided that it would be easier if we just kept our names for business reasons."

Taylor went on, "If you only knew what a mess I was when I met my husband. I was 19 and a student in a class he was teaching. I had no father and lived with my mother on our orange farm. My mother was an alcoholic who entertained some really bad guys. I had to run a farm and go to school.

"I had no friends my own age. My friends were bikers, not to say that there is anything wrong with that, who were ex-military. They saved my life, and I mean that literally.

"I persuaded my now husband to help me with a kidnapping case involving a little girl for whom I babysat. We worked on the case and its aftermath for several years. I went on to college and law school, with his encouragement. He always encouraged me to do what was best for me, and not for him. I think that was what really made me fall in love with him."

"What does he do?"

"He is a senior trial deputy in the DA's office in Haven. We have a beautiful home and a beautiful life together. I am truly blessed."

"I hope that I can find someone like that."

Taylor said, "I am not the type of person who likes to give advice about matters of the heart, but I will tell you this. When you are looking for someone to share your life with, look for a person of substance, someone who puts your needs above his and who can take care of himself and you, if that becomes necessary. Do not go for the pretty, bad boy ogled by all of the girls. That will only leave you alone or alone with a child."

"It's hard. The bad boys look so good. But I hear you. Girls are often not looking very far down the road when making life-long decisions."

Taylor went on, "My husband had an idyllic home life with a mother who was a doctor and a father who was a lawyer. They both showered him with love and opportunity.

"I asked him once if he ever asked his mother why she chose his father, as she was, by all accounts, beautiful, particularly when she was young.

"He said that his mother told him that she chose his father because she thought that he would be a great father and a good provider. I must confess that until I heard this story, I never thought that either of those things would ever be important. Boy was I wrong."

Amanda replied, "That is great advice. I too would never have considered either to be important. I have always been looking for the handsome bad boy."

Taylor changed the subject again, "What brought you to the AG's office?"

Amanda replied, "I was hoping to work in white collar crime, particularly environmental law. Going to school with mostly tree-huggers, I have been indoctrinated with maintaining the environment. I'm not certain that environmental law will be available to me here in this office, but I need to start somewhere."

Taylor submitted, "Here in Fairview the environmental law section is quite small. I don't know if I am exactly at liberty to say this, but the State has created an environmental task force, and I'm the designee from our office. If it really interests you, I can put in a word. Personal interest often helps to achieve professional results.

"I find it curious that the conservative segment of our population opposes environmental laws and regulations. I guess the feeling is that if the large corporations are not held to environmental standards, they will be able to produce more goods and services for less money, thereby maintaining the economic status quo of allowing the rich to get richer.

"The public relations from our side is sorely lacking. When toxic waste is allowed into the water, it is delivered downstream, gets into the soil and wildlife, and contaminates our water and food.

"As important as contamination is, the connection between the contamination and the onset of injuries can be lengthy and difficult to prove.

"As a result, my focus has been directed to situations where environmental crimes lead to more immediate injuries or death, as in these cases the cause and effect may be possible to prove.

"I don't discount contamination and its effects, but there are only so many hours in the day, and chasing injury caused by contamination might be too difficult to prove. So, I have been forced to direct my resources to more immediate injuries, such as those from exposure to toxic substances.

"We have situations where CEOs will order the illegal disposal of toxic waste. During the illegal dumping, contact with the illegal substance may cause one or more people to die. Believe it or not, for the death, the perpetrators will be charged with involuntary manslaughter, which does not carry much of a penalty. Also, often the charges will be brought against rank and file workers and not against the CEOs, officers, and high-level managers who actually order the dumping and who benefit from it.

"Recently, I broached this with my task force boss on the theory that in such cases, the charge should be second degree murder and should include everyone all the way up to the CEO. This is the only way we will deter this conduct. Otherwise, it is cheaper for the company to break the law and pay the fines, allowing the low-level managers or rank and file workers to twist in the wind."

Amanda responded, "I see your dilemma. Maybe I should go for a less controversial sub-specialty. Environmental sounds too complicated and dangerous."

Taylor chimed in, "I don't disagree with you. But to really get something worthwhile done, you have to go after the big fish, even if there is an element of danger. I just can't help myself. I drive my husband a little crazy with this. And I really don't want to get in a situation where I cannot be totally truthful with him."

Amanda said, "I see. It's a major problem. Well, I don't have to make my decision right away. Anyway, I doubt that I could get into the environmental section, even if I wanted it.

Taylor replied, "Why don't we see how things develop before making any earth-shattering decisions. We can talk about how things are progressing and see if it would be a good fit for you."

"When do I get to meet this husband of yours?"

"He is going on a camping trip oddly enough with some friends of mine. He'll be gone for a week, and I'll be on my own. This should give us a chance to meet a couple of more times this week, if that's okay with you?"

"That would be great. Camping?"

"It's not exactly camping. It's more like survivalist training. He will go up in the mountains with some of my ex-military friends, and they will show him how to use a gun, how to fight, and stuff like that. I did it myself eight years ago. It was a great experience and taught me a great deal about defending myself.

"It was around the time that I was working on the kidnapping case of the little girl for whom I babysat. While trying to get a better look at the compound where we believed the little girl was being held, I was captured and imprisoned myself. Rick and my ex-military friends staged a daring rescue against the kidnapper, his body guards, and a para-military group he kept on retainer and rescued me and the little girl.

"So, Rick will be with my ex-military friends learning valuable things. I heard that in addition to shooting and fighting, they are also going to a location where a mock office tower complete with an advanced security system has been erected to train for urban warfare. Sounds fun. I sort of wish I was going, but I am new to this job and prefer to not take time off right now, and, anyway, I do not want to distract Rick."

Amanda exclaimed, "Wow. You guys take this stuff seriously."

"Yes, we do."

Taylor walked Amanda out to her car. They made quite a pair.

When they arrived at Amanda's car, Amanda opened the door. Taylor said that she had a nice time. Amanda said the same.

Amanda continued, "Let's agree to be friends and try to support one another. From the sounds of things, you will be ruffling some feathers and will need a friend."

Taylor replied, "That is very true. Let's hope that this friendship of ours will hold up during the trying times ahead."

Chapter Twelve
Camping

Rick agreed to meet Moose, Bart, Lester, and some of Moose's other friends at the north entrance to Rock Ridge National Park. This was the same location to which Rick was sent by Taylor to find Moose when she was apprehended and imprisoned at the compound where she thought Tammy was being held. No fond memories for Rick here.

As before, Rick was directed to the parking lot where he would leave his vehicle and then hike to the camping area.

After Rick reached the camping area, Moose asked him why he felt it was necessary for him to learn survival skills at all. Moose reasoned that he and Taylor were safe now. They were both employed and living comfortably.

Moose asked Rick, "Why don't you and Taylor just get on with your lives and let law enforcement take care of your security?"

Rick replied, "I feel that I owe it to myself and to Taylor to be more prepared than I was when she was being held. I really felt powerless. If she had to rely on me and I didn't have you and your guys for help, it might have been worse. This is something I have to do."

Moose continued, "I get all that, but do you think that you are really cut out to defend yourself in any meaningful way? Taylor is a farm girl. She comes from a messed-up family and had to learn from a very young age how to protect herself. She had to run a farm, fix the plumbing, irrigate the land, and take care of sick animals, which I am sure included putting a few down. She was up at three in the morning burning smudge when the weather threatened to damage the orange crops.

"I have no doubt that if I came at Taylor meaning to do her harm, she would shoot me between the eyes and finish me off with two taps to the chest without a second's hesitation.

"She may look like an upper-middle-class lady now, but under that thin veneer, she is still a hunter, and, my friend, in the end, hunters hunt. If you are unable to do what we need here, we are wasting our time."

The thing about Moose is that on more than one occasion he has been very critical of me, but he has always been so directly to my face. None of that behind the back BS for him. But I have never been able to get mad at him because he has always been honest, and generally right. I never fault someone for telling the truth, regardless of how much it hurts.

Rick concluded, "Moose, I thank you for the admonition, but this is something I have to do."

Moose closed with, "Okay, we will do the gun and fight training here and then go to the other location for the building-assault training."

My first assignment was with Bart. We would hike to an upper clearing where the light was good. I remember hearing from Taylor that just getting to the clearing was a rough hike. After barely making it up there myself that might qualify as an understatement. For Bart, however, it was barely a stroll.

I had seen Bart in action during the rescue of Taylor from the compound. I will never forget how he thrust his hand through a tiny opening in the door and grabbed that a-hole by the throat with so much force that it scared even me.

Bart said that most of the techniques are part of an attack plan known as Krav Magi. This means basically that there are no rules.

The first move I was shown was the kick to the groin. Though outlawed in almost any civilized society, this is a favored method in Krav Magi. As Bart so aptly explained, the rules are one thing for competitive sport fighting, but when one is fighting for his life, there are no rules.

We moved to the eye gouge. This is where two fingers penetrate into the eye socket, and the eyeball is pulled and damaged.

We then moved to the elbow block. When one comes at you with a right cross, you slide your left arm inside of his right arm to block his punch. This opens his face which you immediately punch with your right hand.

Bart then showed me the long and the short knee. With the long knee, the knee is thrust up into the opponent's abdomen. With the short knee, the knee is thrust up into the opponent's face. Both moves are done while holding onto the opponent's neck, and either move could be followed with an elbow to the Adam's apple.

Interestingly enough, the punching and other attacks are generally directed towards the throat and not to the face or stomach, as one might expect. The throat protects the windpipe which is quite vulnerable and therefore becomes the target of several moves.

Two different stomping techniques were shown for situations when the opponent has been driven to the ground. The groin or knee may be stomped with the bottom of the foot coming from a bent leg or from the heel when coming from a straight leg. The straight leg stomp is known as an ax stomp.

The nutcracker choke is actually aimed at the Adam's apple and not below the belt. Apparently, the Adam's apple is relatively vulnerable.

Last, but not least, was the fish hook. One could grab his opponent's mouth and eye and pull the face, avoiding being bitten by the teeth.

We then spent a great deal of time working on weapons take away. Bart taught me to step away from the barrel of the gun before forcing it away from the assailant. It was a quick move that would be coupled with some of the other self-defense techniques he already showed me. He said that it was very dangerous. But if you are going to be shot anyway, why not at least give it a try.

Bart and I worked on these moves for two hours. Though he was being as gentle as possible, I was still pretty beaten up at the end. However, with his patient teaching, I learned much.

We made the hike back to the campground. Fortunately, the way back was not as bad as the way up.

When we arrived, it was time to start preparing dinner. As Taylor had told me, everyone worked, regardless of seniority, age, or ability.

We prepared a meal of barbequed short ribs, corn, and potatoes from a frozen bag of hash browns. After dinner, we shared some fruit. No alcohol, which was fine with me since I didn't drink much anyway.

We cleared the dinner tables, cleaned the dishes, pots and pans, and the cooking utensils, and retired to our sleeping areas. The night was warm. I slept in a sleeping bag outside. Some slept in tents, and others, including Moose, Bart, and Lester, slept outside.

The next morning, we awoke and got breakfast ready. After breakfast, we cleared the dishes and cleaned the eating area. We were ready for the day.

Today, I would go with Lester and learn about guns. Something about which I knew nothing.

Lester and I hiked up the trail along the river. It was a much less rigorous hike than the hike with Bart the day before. We found a clearing and some room for target practice.

Lester said he would start with gun ownership and licensing. He said that a person had to be 18 to purchase a long gun and 21 to purchase a handgun. Handgun purchases also required proof of residence. It will take a minimum of 10 days before you can leave the store with your gun.

All gun purchases require the purchasers to possess a Firearm Safety Certificate (FSC). To obtain an FSC, one must receive a score of 75 percent on the FSC test covering firearm safety and basic firearms law.

Some people are prohibited from purchasing or possessing a firearm if they have been convicted of a felony or some of the more serious domestic violence misdemeanors.

California law allows one to possess a gun at his place of business or residence. If a gun owner knows or should know that a minor or other person not qualified to possess a gun could access the gun, the gun must be in a locked container.

If one wishes to carry a concealed weapon, he must first obtain permission from the local police department or sheriff.

Lester then proceeded to shooting technique. Generally, handguns are gripped with two hands with the dominant hand on the bottom providing the trigger finger and the other hand over the dominant hand. Both thumbs are pointed forward.

There are two different stances, the Weaver Stance and the Isosceles Stance.

With the Weaver Stance, the support foot is forward, and the dominant foot is angled to the side. The front knee is bent slightly, and the back leg is straight. The dominant arm is pointed straight from the right eye, and the support arm is bent at the elbow, with the support hand below the dominant hand.

With the Isosceles Stance, the feet are shoulder width apart, both knees are bent, and both arms are held straight, locked at the elbows. In this stance, the shooter faces the target straight on.

The trigger finger rests on the trigger in the center of the last pad and not at the joint or tip.

It is nearly impossible to hold the gun perfectly still. The idea is that with practice the wobble should become smaller.

We set up a target. Lester brought along a Glock. He thought it was more accurate than a Colt. He took a couple of shots. Wow, he blew the center out of the target.

He got me up in the Isosceles Stance. My elbows were locked. I sighted down from my right eye and pulled the trigger. Let's just say that it was a long afternoon. After an hour I finally hit somewhere close to the target. As time progressed, I got better. I could see much practice in my future.

At least I knew how to shoot. This alone was worth the few hours spent.

Lester and I returned to the camp. It was dinner time. We helped prepare food along with Moose, Bart, and the other guys. We cleaned up and went to bed.

The next day we woke up and made a large breakfast. There were pancakes, eggs, bacon, potatoes, and coffee.

Everyone began packing their belongings. I followed suit, not knowing exactly what the schedule was going to be. I drove myself, so I had my car in the lot.

We all hiked down to the lot. Moose came over to me and told me that he and the other guys decided to forego the urban training class. He said that he needed to get back to work and that the other guys lost interest. But he said that I could go on without them, if I wished. I had already been cleared for another couple of days with work, so I decided to go do the urban training by myself.

Besides, now I could rent a motel room and get a shower and a good night's sleep.

We were both fine with it. The guys left on their motorcycles, and I left in my Suburban, going in the opposite direction.

According to the map, I would proceed west on the interstate, turn south on I-87, and exit on Lincoln. Everyone said that once I reached the exit that I would be able to see my destination from the highway.

Chapter Thirteen
Urban Training

I rambled along I-87 for several miles. I then saw the sign that included Lincoln as an off-ramp, two and three-quarter miles ahead. After traveling two miles, I could see that of which everyone was speaking.

To the right of the freeway, there was what appeared to be a tall glass wall. The wall was constructed similar to one wall of a corporate-type office building with glass panels connected by metal cross bars. The ground floor and two additional floors fit in behind the one full height (10 stories) front glass wall.

I exited the highway and saw the entrance for the parking garage. The parking garage was a three-story concrete structure adjacent to the glass walled building.

I entered the parking garage and was directed by the parking attendant to the adjoining building with its one glass wall. He told me to enter through the front door, and there would be a receptionist who would direct me further.

I parked, walked across a landscaped outdoor patio, opened the front door, and entered the building. Upon entry, I could see that the lobby appeared similar to the entry lobby of a typical corporate office building, including a long counter with four computer stations. Three people, two women and one man, were standing behind three of the four terminals.

Towards the perimeter of the lobby, on the left side of the reception counter, there was a mock security desk. This desk was manned by someone appearing more as a security person. If someone entered the building and did not know where he was going, he would report to the reception desk from where he would be directed to the security desk or asked to leave the premises.

If someone entered the building either through the front door or from the mock elevator from the parking garage and knew where he was going, such as a tenant, he would go directly to the security desk.

Everyone entering the building, whether a visitor or a tenant, would be required to sign in at the security desk to gain access to the first-floor offices or to the elevator to the upper floors.

If someone entered the building with a delivery, he would leave the package with a receptionist.

It did not take a genius to figure out that the entry, entry lobby, reception desk, security desk, hallway, and the first-floor offices were designed to appear similar to a typical corporate office building. There was even an elevator attached to the free-standing glass wall which one would enter from the faux lobby.

I made-contact with one of the receptionists. She said that they were expecting four people. I told her that the other three people needed to return home and that they sent me along by myself. She called a co-worker and explained that some of my party was not with me. She was told that I could attend the class by myself.

I was sent to the faux security desk where I was checked in. I was given a visitor's badge and was sent to Suite 104 located behind the reception desk.

The inside of Suite 104 appeared similar to many of the offices I had visited over the years. It had a reception area of its own with a sliding window behind which the receptionist and clerical staff did their business.

I checked in with the Suite 104 receptionist. She asked me to take a seat in the suite's reception area, which I did.

After a few minutes, a young lady opened the reception area door and asked me to come with her. We entered a hallway inside of the suite which lead to several offices. I was taken to the far corner office. She opened the door and allowed me into the private office of Mr. Baldwin.

Mr. Baldwin said, "Hello, you must be someone from the motorcycle club. My name is David Baldwin."

"Yes. Something like that. My name is Rick Miller. I'm an attorney with the Haven DA's office and a guest lecturer at Newton Junior College. But I am associated with the motorcycle club of which you spoke."

Mr. Baldwin continued, "I understand that you are here for the urban assault training."

"Yes. That is correct."

"Very good then. It's getting a little late in the day to get started. Why don't you get a motel room and report back to the main reception area tomorrow morning at 8 a.m.?"

I replied, "Okay. I will be back here then."

I left his office, found my way back to my car, and headed out of the parking area looking for a motel. There were several motels along Lincoln past the building. I found one that looked relatively clean and drove in. I parked, went to the front office, registered, was given a key to room 8. I walked to room 8 and opened the door.

The room was decent but clearly not lavish. The last time I was in a motel room I was with my now wife before we got married. I do not think that this experience will be anything similar to that one.

I brought in my bag, took a quick shower, and went to bed. I asked for a 6 o'clock wake-up call.

The wake-up call came at 6. I had enough time to grab a cup of tea and a piece of toast, get dressed, and get to the Urban Assault training center by 8.

Upon arriving, I checked in at the security desk. I was directed to the outdoor staging area behind the building. There I met Hank Greenberg, who appeared to be my instructor.

Mr. Greenberg was a mature man around 50. He looked pretty seasoned and a little weathered, as one might expect, and hope.

I explained that the rest of my party would not be in attendance. He said he knew but that we were going to proceed anyway.

He told me that he was a former Army Ranger and was happy to have a job doing something he both liked and knew.

He explained that we were going to learn the things necessary to breech a tall building. He said that we were going to learn how to scale the outside, break into the com room, disable coms, detain the security guards and office staff, and do all things necessary to extract hostages, if any.

We started with scaling the building. Mr. Greenberg told me that many attempts to scale tall buildings had been made, mostly with suction cups, because most tall buildings were now made of glass with metal framing.

He said that a suction cup is typically pressed against a glass surface with the center being depressed all of the way to the glass. This would force the air out from inside of the cup which makes for a better grip. He said that the typical suction cup was designed for moving glass and not for holding the weight of a person.

Some suction cups had hand pumps. The pump would force the air out from the inside of the cup. This was better than a strictly manual cup but was not recommended for climbing.

A young lady had recently scaled a tall building using suction cups attached to two vacuum cleaners. When the cup was pressed against the glass, the vacuum would suck the air out of the cup for a more-firm grip. Compressed air could be used similarly. It might be possible to scale a building with these techniques. Also, water can be used for this purpose.

I was hooked up with a safety rope to the top of the glass wall. I started a slow ascent up the side of the building. It went pretty well, and I was able to make it to the top. Once at the top, I let myself down on the rope.

The next part of my instruction concerned the building's internal surveillance. We started in the lobby. As noted before, the lobby has a long desk with four computer terminals. During the shifts, one or more of the terminals is manned. The lobby was set up to appear similar to a lobby one might find in an urban high rise.

My instructor advised me that rather than storming the reception area, it might be best to hold off as long as possible. This was due to the sheer size of a high rise building and the time it takes to move from one part of the building to the other.

One would presume that if there were bad actors in the building, they would be near the penthouse, or on the upper floors, or on the roof where an escape helicopter could land. The penthouse would be the most likely place where one might find the real decision maker, such as the CEO.

If one could talk his way past the receptionists, he would have more time to reach the penthouse without attracting attention, which would probably be better than he might do with force alone.

My instructor told me that it was more likely that one would need to take over the security room and all of the security guards. In a private home or small office building, the security monitors might be located in the office of the owner. In a high-rise building, however, the monitors would most likely be located in a security room where the hired security staff would be located. It is unlikely that a CEO would watch the monitors himself.

After the initial contact with the reception desk, one would have to locate the security room, which is typically located on the first floor, near the rear of the building.

Before breaching the door of the security room, one would have to round up and restrain all of the receptionists for two reasons. Firstly, they could notify others, including the on-site security staff. Secondly, their biological information might be necessary to enter the security room. One might need to take a receptionist to have his or her eye or fingerprint scanned to gain access to the security room.

My instructor advised me that it would probably be necessary to replace at least one of the receptionists with one or more of your own people. Depending upon the skill and acting ability of the person chosen, he or she might be able to hold off casual visitors and delivery people and even some of the less informed security people, allowing the mission to continue uninterrupted.

Once the security room is breeched, all of its staff, including the guards, would have to be restrained and placed in a holding area along with the receptionists.

Our people would then take over the computers and monitors without anyone else in the building even being aware of a change. This is why the move against the reception desk and security room required subtle action rather than violence.

After the receptionists and security room people were tied up and placed into a locked room, the mission, whatever it turned out to be, could be carried on without the knowledge of the CEO or other security people.

We took a break for lunch. My instructor told me that after lunch, we were going to do some bungee jumping. He did not offer a reason, and I did not ask.

After lunch, we went in my instructor's car to a nearby bridge. There was no water under the bridge this time of year. I worked up the courage to ask about bungee jumping. He said that sometimes, in a pinch, it became necessary to jump from high places. Though this was highly uncommon, it was better to be safe than sorry.

We tied the bungee cord to the railing of the bridge. He said that in a pinch, the large hook on the cord could be hooked over a railing or other metal component of the building.

He said that increasing or decreasing one's speed during the descent was similar to skydiving. When skydiving, if you are spread eagle, your body will provide more wind resistance, and your speed will decrease. If you are pointed either head first or feet first, your speed will increase.

Some of the very high jumps that have been made include the Royal Gorge Bridge in Colorado Springs at 1053 feet. This would be roughly the equivalent to 88 floors. The Macau Tower in China was a 760-foot jump, roughly 64 floors. The Last Resort in Nepal was a 524-foot jump, roughly 44 floors. By way of comparison, the Empire State Building has 102 floors.

All of this was great to know, but it did not ease my fears.

I put on a vest. We hooked the bungee to the vest. And I jumped, head first. Wow. It was a fast descent. Finally, the bungee reached its full length, and I was catapulted back up into space. With less downward force, the bungee finally backed off, and I was left hanging on its end. I was quite close to the ground at this point, and I was able to free myself and fall to the ground, without incident.

I made several jumps and, by the end, was having a great time. I see why people enjoy this as a hobby.

It was becoming late afternoon. We headed back to the main building. My instructor told me that as part of the training for which I paid, I was allowed to keep my body harness and the bungee cord. I packed both into the back of my Suburban.

I had already checked out of the motel and had all of my stuff in my car. I decided to drive home where I could see that beautiful wife of mine.

When I arrived home my wife asked me how it was. I said that it was very informative and that I particularly liked the bungee jumping, which surprised me.

She asked about bungee jumping. I explained the harness, the cord, the hooks, and the accessories. I told her that one could modulate his or her speed while in the air. If one dove head first or feet first in a more vertical plane, he or she would go faster. To minimize one's speed, one could extend into a spread-eagle position.

I told her about the shooting and hand-to-hand combat, and she seemed favorably impressed. We went to bed to wake up the next morning for work.

Chapter Fourteen
Taylor and Amanda at Work

After Rick returned home, he and Taylor settled into their normal routine. Rick would be working long hours in the DA's office and doing his guest lecturing.

Taylor would continue to work long hours with Amanda, mostly with environmental law issues. Amanda and Taylor were trying to make some headway, but as politics began to drift to the more conservative, environmental law violations were becoming less rigorously enforced.

They did have a few interesting cases. In one case, the Coast Guard found evidence that the crew of a container ship at the Port of Los Angeles was dumping oily bilge water into the sea. The crew worked for Capital Ship Management, a publicly traded company. One would think that prosecutors would go after Capital, as it was the ship's management company.

Instead, prosecutors chose to enter into a non-prosecution agreement not with Capital but with one of its subsidiaries. The subsidiary was allowed to plead guilty, pay a fine, and enter into a compliance program which applied to only one ship. Capital Ship Management avoided criminal liability altogether. Its other ships were free to continue on, business as usual.

In the case of Hardrock Excavating, the owner directed his employees to empty brine from a fracking operation into a waste water drain which ultimately ran to a river. He received 28 months in prison and a $25,000. fine.

Comcast was found to have routinely and systematically allowed hazardous waste in the form of electronic equipment to be placed into local landfills which were not permitted to receive these items. They were assessed nearly 20 million dollars in fines and were required to purchase air time to educate the public. They were also required to institute programs to enhance their ability to remain environmentally compliant.

Taylor and Amanda were reasonably happy with their work, and they were fast becoming rising stars in the office. But Taylor felt that the corporations were becoming more-clever about hiding their polluting activities, and some were allowed to escape criminal penalties altogether.

Taylor again explained to Amanda that it was her mission to extract more compliance from the primary actors. So far, the primary actors had side-stepped the serious penalties by throwing their underlings under the bus. Imagine that.

Chapter Fifteen
Rick's Second Guest Lecture

"In our first discussion, we found that the Constitution set up the three branches of government, prohibited one State from charging duties to another State, provided that all duties collected would belong to the new federal government, and specified that debts incurred prior to the Constitution would be valid against the new federal government after the Constitution.

"During the Washington Administration, what was once theory began to be undertaken as practice.

"Laws would be enacted to raise money through tariffs.

"Alexander Hamilton, as Secretary of the Treasury, would push through Congress his plan for the federal government to use tariffs to both pay the national debt and to assume the States' debts, without an income tax. (This would directly benefit 40 of the 55 founders who owned State debt or what was then known as a public security.)

"The Judiciary Act created the circuit courts, and the district courts. Article III created the Supreme Court. During the Washington Administration, in 1791, the Bill of Rights was ratified.

"Thus, it was during the first Washington Administration that the Constitution's vision of raising money through tariffs to pay the national and States' debts without an income tax was put into actual practice.

"In short, it took the work of the Washington Administration to bring the economic theories set out in the Constitution to actual life.

"Less importantly, as it turns out, Hamilton was also able to push through a national bank. The first and second national banks were not abolished, but their 20-year charters were not renewed.

"The national banks were not the same as the Federal Reserve system that we have in operation today. The national banks did not regulate banking, as the Federal Reserve does. Instead, the national banks were the only banks that were allowed to conduct business interstate, or between states. All other banks were allowed to conduct business only intrastate, only within one state.

"In 1913, the Federal Reserve system revamped the country's financial operation, and this revamping was followed by the income tax. I would submit that the Federal Reserve system was one of the most egregious concentrations of power ever perpetrated on the American public. I believe that the founding fathers would roll over in their graves if they learned that the country was supported by income taxes. But that is only my opinion.

"After George Washington retired from the Presidency, the next election was set for 1796. By this time, less than a dozen years after the ratification of the Constitution, there were already political parties.

"No political parties were mentioned in the Constitution, and they were not favored by the original framers as they were thought to be too divisive. This is a sentiment with which I do not believe anyone in his or her right mind could disagree.

"By the Election of 1796, political parties not only existed, but they were organized well enough to present candidates for President. They presented the Vice-President, John Adams as the Federalist candidate and Thomas Jefferson, the one-time Secretary of State, as the Republican candidate.

"France supported Jefferson, which worked against him and threw the election to John Adams.

"France's refusal to see an American delegation without a sizeable bribe turned America towards war with France. The fact that higher taxes would be needed to support a war lessened the pro war sentiment. Today, money for a war is not even a consideration. Today, we go to war with places such as Viet Nam and Iraq, whether we have the money or not, and when we run out of money, which we invariably do, we print it, leaving us in the debt mess we are in now.

"By 1800, Napoleon Bonaparte was coming into power in France. To consolidate his position at home, he agreed to a treaty with America.

"In an effort to perpetuate their control, the Federalists enacted the Alien and Sedition Acts. The Alien Act made it more difficult to become a naturalized citizen and gave the President the power to deport aliens. The Sedition Act allowed to be punished any person who published a false or malicious statement against the President or Congress.

"These Acts were so unpopular that they brought about the doctrine of nullification under which individual States could seek to nullify acts of the federal Congress. Abridging freedom of speech, in nearly any form, has never been a favored position in the United States.

"The Federalists were so discredited by the Alien and Sedition Acts that Jefferson was elected President in 1800, the first non-Federalist to hold that office.

"The Election of 1800, though it replaced a Federalist with a Republican, did not result in the type of sweeping changes that one might have expected. It did not turn the government over to the people, as advertised. When Jefferson was faced with the reality of actually running the country, his politics tempered, and he drifted more to the center.

"The Election of 1800, rather than creating a democracy, shifted the control of the government from the mercantile aristocracy of the northeast to the agrarian aristocracy of the south and west.

"Under Jefferson, James Madison became Secretary of State.

"The case of Marbury v. Madison gave the Supreme Court the power to declare acts of Congress unconstitutional. In 1803, the Louisiana Purchase was consummated with the Lewis and Clark expedition exploring the new land.

"This brings us to the Election of 1804 in which Jefferson was re-elected in a landslide victory. The Election of 1804 was conducted under the 12th Amendment by which the electors would vote separate ballots, one for President and one for Vice-President.

"Next time we will get into the second Jefferson Administration and the War of 1812.

Rick gathered up his briefcase and went home. It was about 9 p.m., and his wife was up waiting for him.

When he arrived home, she asked, "How did the lecture go?"

Rick replied, "Fine. I don't think anyone was listening. This period in American history is not quite as interesting as some of the others."

"I'm sure that everyone loved the information. Have you eaten?"

"No. I was just going to make something."

Rick made himself a sandwich. Taylor, who had already eaten, sat with him while he ate. After dinner, he cleaned up the kitchen, and they both went off to bed.

Rick asked, "What's up for tomorrow?"

Taylor replied, "Just the usual stuff. I should be in the office most of the day."

"Okay. I'll see you in the morning."

Rick shut off the lights and joined his wife in bed.

Chapter Sixteen
The Fairview Office of the Attorney General

A youngish, good-looking gentleman entered the reception area for the Fairview Office of the Attorney General.

He was well dressed in business-like attire. He looked to be in his late thirties. He appeared prosperous.

He addressed the receptionist, "Hello, my name is Trey St. James. I have a 9 o'clock appointment with Mr. Patterson. Is he available?"

The receptionist said, "He's in his office. Allow me to call him."

She picked up the telephone receiver and pressed an intercom button. This rang directly to Mr. Patterson. She told him that there was a Trey St. James at reception to see him. He said that he would come out.

It appeared as if the receptionist paid a little more attention to Mr. St. James than she might have to one of the office's normal visitors as he was quite good looking and dashing, and she wanted to make a favorable impression.

Mr. Patterson came out of a door which lead from the hallway into the reception area. He was coming from his personal office.

Once he was visible, the receptionist stated, "This gentleman is here for his 9 o'clock appointment."

Mr. Patterson asked Trey to follow him. They went back through the same door, the same hallway, and into the private office of Mr. Patterson.

Mr. Patterson moved behind his desk and sat down. He motioned for his visitor to sit in a large chair opposite his desk.

Once seated Mr. Patterson said, "You must be the investigator they told me they were sending down from the Sacramento office. I spoke with Mr. Deaver, and he asked me to extend to you the full courtesy of this office, which I intend to do."

Trey replied, "Thank you."

Mr. Patterson went on, "They told me that they were planning to send someone to help our lawyers with some of the more high-profile environmental cases, just in case there are any problems with the companies being investigated."

Mr. Patterson continued, "It has gotten to the point where hazardous waste disposal has become so expensive that some companies might find it tempting to cut some corners, if you know what I mean. With many of these companies their security staff can get pretty aggressive trying to protect off book dumping or other violations.

"Two of my young female deputies have taken on some of these cases, and they can get pretty inquisitive."

Mr. Trey interjected, "Yes. Sometimes people who are given a little bit of power can get to feeling indestructible."

Mr. Patterson continued, "I don't think that this is the case with these two. They are both pretty careful, but one can never be too vigilant. In that vein, it might be a good idea if, along with your other duties here, you could just sort of keep an eye them for me."

Trey responded, "No problem. I will keep an eye on them."

Mr. Patterson went on, "The two deputies of whom I am speaking are Taylor Shaw and Amanda Warren. Taylor is the senior of the two and is also part of the State environmental task force which Mr. Deaver heads out of Sacramento. I am sure that you will meet them during your work here.

"I will arrange an office for you. I was not told how long your assignment would to run. I guess we will figure that out as we go."

Trey responded, "Sounds good. Just point me in the direction of my office, and I will get out of your hair."

"I'll do you one better. I'll take you there myself."

Mr. Patterson escorted Trey down the hall to an empty office.

"This will be your office."

Trey looked over the office. It had a desk, two chairs, a couch, and some bookshelves. It was not fancy, but it was adequate.

"Thank you, Mr. Patterson. This should do nicely."

On one wall, there was a window which looked out onto a park. It was a nice view.

Mr. Patterson returned to his office. He thought over the addition of an investigator to his staff. His initial impression of Trey was that he was probably very popular in school. He was probably an athlete. He appeared to be the type of person who made friends easily and who is fairly aggressive with people generally.

He's a good-looking guy and is probably very good with the ladies. Mr. Patterson was thinking to himself that this might do him some good with Amanda but would probably not serve him particularly well with Taylor.

Trey was a flashy dresser. He was accessorized with jewelry. He drove a fancy car. He generally appeared to be more prosperous than one might expect on an investigator's salary. Mr. Patterson was certain that Trey's outward appearance of prosperity was part of his job and that the clothes and car were probably part of the cover given to him by the State of California for his work.

From the excellence of Taylor's work, Mr. Patterson thought that she might see through Trey. Even so, he thought that it would be very unlikely that Trey could be of any real harm.

Investigators for the OCI are duly sworn peace officers and, as such, are authorized to make arrests and carry firearms. Having such a person on staff, overall, would probably be of some benefit.

Amanda, Taylor, Mr. Patterson, and the rest of the office staff were told only that Trey was an investigator assigned to help them out, as needed, which, to them, appeared he was.

Even Mr. Patterson was not told of Trey's actual job. Trey's stated job was to act as an investigator for Mr. Patterson's entire office. However, his actual job was to work for Mr. Deaver. His actual job was to insinuate himself into the work of Amanda and Taylor in order to make certain that they did not get too close to any of the possible wrongdoings of any of Mr. Deaver's outside corporate clients.

Trey was cleaver. He started slow. He invited Amanda for coffee, a move not endorsed by womanizers anywhere. They took walks outside around the office, and he appeared to show a legitimate interest in her. She was attractive but not overly showy. Just perfect for his purposes.

They went out on a couple of real dates, and after three dates, things started to get pretty hot and heavy. Trey was not above exploiting his professional targets for sex.

Taylor had little to do with him. As Mr. Patterson surmised, she saw through him almost immediately.

Amanda, on the other hand, was quite smitten. He was a good-looking guy and gave off that bad boy vibe that often intrigues women in general and Amanda in particular. He had the outward appearance of prosperity with the clothes and the car. This too never hurts with the ladies.

Chapter Seventeen
The Bar Downstairs

There is a bar downstairs in the office building. Though it has a name, the "Redwood Room," it may as well have been named the "bar downstairs," as that is what it is referred to by everyone.

Prior to the arrival of Trey, Taylor and Amanda met regularly after working hours and almost always at the bar downstairs. They would talk about the several cases they were working on, sharing intelligence and evidence. They had developed a nice teacher-student type relationship which was good for both of them.

Taylor enjoyed teaching and had much to teach. Amanda, who was new to the practice, enjoyed learning and had much to learn in many arenas, both in work and in life.

Taylor explained her formative years to Amanda with no father, an alcoholic mother, men chasing her, her ties to a motorcycle gang, the kidnapping of the little girl, her mission to recover the girl, meeting Rick, recovering the little girl, and how meeting Rick set her on the path to college, law school, this job, and, finally, marriage.

Taylor generally kept the description of her early life short and not too detailed as, in point of actual fact, she was not proud of her circumstances. She preferred to focus on her life after meeting Rick and their life together, something more meaningful. She fought the demons of her less than perfect upbringing.

Rick, with all of the advantages of a wonderful home with two loving parents and every opportunity was so patient and gentle with Taylor, allowing her to find her own way in the world without forcing her to be one way or the other.

His methods worked beautifully, and Taylor began to adopt as much of his ability to care for others as she could.

Amanda explained her own childhood. She also had two loving parents. Her father was a successful insurance broker, and her mother did some real estate sales work when she could. They tried to offer her every advantage including private schools and, ultimately, Stanford University, which was quite significant.

Her time at Stanford allowed her to meet the children of many influential people and elevated her to a position perhaps higher than the position her parents achieved. This was one of the many benefits of attending a top school. Access to people with money and influence.

Graduating from Stanford Law School, Amanda had the opportunity to work for any of the most prestigious law firms in the country. She would be in a position to earn a large salary and to receive investment advice from clients to compound her earnings.

She opted instead to work for the State Attorney General. This was far from a glamorous job and was a job available to graduates from lesser law schools, such as Taylor's.

Amanda was pretty smart about some things. She would never demean anyone who came from a lesser background, school, or circumstance than she. She was smart enough to know that she obtained her position, at least partly, from the accident of birth and not necessarily from being the smartest person in the room.

Taylor was impressed with Amanda's way of not looking down on people. But she had no first-hand knowledge about Amanda's attitude about, for example, men.

Taylor and Amanda met in the bar downstairs to discuss some of their cases. After talking shop briefly, Amanda asked,

"What do you think of Trey?"

Taylor replied, "Truthfully? I don't think about him at all."

Amanda asked, "Don't you think he's cute?"

Taylor replied, "No. And I'm married. But even if I were not married, I would not find him the least bit attractive. In my opinion, he is all of the things I dislike about men."

"What do you mean?"

Taylor started, "He's arrogant, self-absorbed, cocky, and phony. He does not seem to me to be particularly well read and has nothing interesting to say, both of which are more important to me than looks. He might fool many women with his act. Every girl wants to tame a bad-boy.

"You have to remember Amanda that when I was just a girl I was exposed to the real thing, real-bad-boys, and not just to want-to-be bad-boys like Trey. And I can tell you with certainty that they are not only a pain in the ass, but they are also dangerous, both emotionally and sometimes even physically. And I plan on never putting myself in that position again. I was already put in that position with some real bad characters by my mother, and, frankly, I'm done with it.

"When I went looking for a man, I, by the grace of God, found a real man. A man who leads his life for me. A man who really cares about me. Unfortunately, Trey will never be that person because all he cares about is himself."

Taylor continued, "I see how you look at him around the office. I've been told that you two are dating, and I did not even ask or wish to be told. I would never pretend to tell you what to do for yourself. I like you a great deal, and I firmly believe that you have great potential as a lawyer and as a person. Believe me when I say that I would not have spent the kind of time with you that I have unless I felt that way.

"But what you do with Trey will have to be your own decision to make. I cannot make it for you. I can only tell you how I feel."

Amanda looked a little shocked.

The room was well set up for married people to carry on extra-marital affairs. It was intentionally dark, and the booths had high backs so that the people sitting in the booth could only be seen from the front. The front of the booths opened into a fairly wide infield which was very, very dark, obscuring the view even from just across the room.

Couples could rendezvous in these booths and never be seen. If an unsuspecting spouse should come into the restaurant, the staff was directed to take the spouse to another part of the restaurant.

As Taylor and Amanda sat at the back of a booth, none other than Trey came in. He was brought over to their booth.

Taylor was surprised, but she did not show it.

Amanda said, "Hi Trey. I'm glad you could come by."

She then said to Taylor, "I hope you don't mind, but I asked Trey to join me here thinking that you and I would be finished with our business by this time."

Taylor replied, "No problem. I was just leaving."

Amanda said, "Could you stay here and keep Trey company until I get back from the restroom?"

"Okay," was Taylor's response.

Trey and Taylor sat in the booth. Taylor was not comfortable. Trey began to try to make small-talk. He then broached a more serious subject.

Trey said, "I hear that you and Amanda are going after some very large corporations about their waste dumping. You know that you have to be careful. These are the big boys, and they can play very rough?"

Taylor responded, "Yes. And if I planned on being afraid of the blowback I might get from the large corporations that I am investigating, I would be selling shoes in a department store rather than working in the environmental division of the State Attorney General's Office. Further, I don't plan on working for one of our large corporate defendants at some time in the future, as many of my colleagues do, so I have no worries."

Trey said, "The blowback, as you call it, might be more dangerous than you believe. You could get physically hurt, or worse."

Taylor said, "Is that a threat? What exactly are your duties for the Attorney General? Are you here to help us charge companies with violations or are you here to persuade us to allow them to continue to break the law, as they done for many years?"

Trey was pretty clever in his own right. He could see that Taylor was not dumb and that she may have figured out his true intentions already. This made him a little bit angry with himself. He wondered whether he had blown his own cover. Or was Taylor she just fishing. Whatever he was thinking, he never let on that she might be onto him.

Trey replied, "I didn't mean anything bad. I just wanted to warn you that there is an element of danger in investigating a major corporation."

He then proceeded to lay out a line BS that he thought would convince her that he only had her best interest at heart.

He said, "I care about you. I don't want to see you or Amanda get hurt."

Taylor appeared unimpressed.

Trey, being a seasoned womanizer, tried the only move he felt he had left in his arsenal, approaching Taylor as a woman. Under the table, he put his hand on Taylor's bare leg thinking that this would make her feel desired by someone as rich and handsome as he, which would bring her to his side.

Oh my, what a colossal mistake.

She quickly pushed his hand off of her leg. She then said briskly, "Come with me."

Just a few feet away, they went through two swinging doors which lead into the hallway for the two bathrooms. The hallway was empty.

Taylor quickly and viciously grabbed Trey's right arm and pinned it against his back. Though he was bigger and probably stronger, Taylor knew how to fight, and she was pissed.

She pushed him up against the wall.

She said, "If you ever so much as touch me again, even by accident, I will break your right arm in three places, and you will have to learn how to write with your left hand.

"I am not going to tell Amanda, Mr. Patterson, Mr. Deaver, or anyone else about our little chat, but I expect you to be on your best behavior from here on out. Got that? And if you do anything to hurt Amanda, either emotionally or, God forbid, physically, I will bring down a reign of terror on you that I promise you will never forget. I am going to leave now. You can go back to the table or leave; your choice."

Just then Amanda came out of the ladies' room and entered the hallway where Taylor and Trey were speaking.

"Hey guys, I didn't expect to see you here. What's up?"

Thinking quickly, Taylor said, "We both needed to use the restroom and just ended up here when you came out. I'm going home now. I'll see you tomorrow at the office."

"See you tomorrow then. Hope everything is okay."

Taylor said, "Everything's fine. No worries. Goodnight."

Taylor went through the double doors, picked up her purse at the booth, and left the restaurant.

Amanda returned to the booth. Trey joined her after finishing in the men's room.

Once they were seated, Amanda said, "Hope everything is alright."

"Yes. No worries. I think I'll be going home now too. I'll see you tomorrow at the office."

"You don't want to come over?"

"Not tonight honey. Maybe another time."

Trey left the table and then the restaurant and returned to his apartment, a little shaken by the wrath of Taylor Shaw.

Chapter Eighteen
The Next Day at the Office

The next day at the office things seemed to return to normal. It was pretty obvious that Taylor did not like Trey but recognized that they were going to have to work together. Her intention was to allow Amanda to make her own decision about him.

The three of them had several facilities in the area to inspect. Most of their inspections concerned toxic waste dumping, as technically Trey was with the enforcement division of the DTSC.

Their first order of business was to check the various companies for EPA ID numbers. A hazardous waste EPA ID number is issued either by the federal EPA or the State DTSC to hazardous waste handlers.

The ID number identifies each handler on the hazardous waste manifest and enables the regulators to track the waste from its origin to its final disposal. This allows the waste to be tracked from the "cradle to the grave."

A waste generator must have an ID number before a transporter will accept his waste for shipment. All hazardous waste transporters and disposal facilities must have their own, separate ID number.

Permanent EPA ID numbers can be either State or federal. In California, State numbers are issued to companies which dispose of less waste than some other companies. The companies that dispose of more waste are required to have a federal number.

Taylor, Amanda, and Trey set out investigating several companies.

They found some smaller cosmetics manufacturers committing hazardous waste violations.

They found a waste hauler discharging marine diesel oil into a storm drain the outfall end of which unloaded into the Los Angeles River.

They found that a company which was permitted to store up to 20,000 gallons of used oil in two above-ground tanks was committing a violation by storing more than the permitted amount.

They were, in effect, doing their job. Even though Taylor and Trey did not particularly like one another, at least on Taylor's end, she felt that the working relationship was adequate. Trey did his job and allowed the women to do theirs. They all received complimentary reviews for their work.

After a few weeks, Trey called Mr. Deaver to let him know how things were progressing and to assure him that nothing of interest was taking place.

Mr. Deaver told him that he had no problem with the routine inspections. He said that he would only be concerned if there was extensive property damage, serious injury, or death during an illegal transportation or disposal.

His fear was that Taylor was such a loose cannon that she might take a serious injury or death to the authorities and seek criminal penalties, and he did not want any of his "special" clients to be subjected to a police investigation. Big companies could not afford the bad press.

Over and above his salary at the AG's office, Mr. Deaver was being paid handsomely by a few large corporations to cover up or derail investigations into their illegal conduct, particularly if the conduct resulted in serious injury or death.

Trey was technically being paid by the State of California to act as an investigator. However, Mr. Deaver had his corporate clients also pay Trey on the side so that he would remain available to help him with his work. This is how Trey was able to finance his wardrobe, car, and apartment, which he could never afford on his State salary.

Mr. Deaver was in a delicate position. He knew that he could not bribe Taylor. She didn't care about money. The only way he had to control the situation was to place Trey in her inner circle and hope that the assignments that she received would continue to be routine. If something other than a routine assignment came in, Deaver would rely on Trey to diffuse the investigation, or otherwise throw Taylor off the track.

Mr. Deaver knew that Taylor was already trying to pressure the office to be more aggressive with the criminal prosecutions particularly trying to elevate deaths occurring during violations from involuntary manslaughter to murder in the second degree.

He had to keep Taylor in the field because she was the only woman he had who was sufficiently qualified, and the office needed to maintain at least the outward appearance of diversity.

In his mind, his ace in all of this was Trey. He knew he could count on Trey to either make sure that Taylor did not learn of a serious injury or death related to one of his corporate clients or to somehow persuade her to not seek severe criminal sanctions.

Taylor, Amanda, and Trey continued to investigate cases. They investigated a case where a pest control company directed its employees to use outdoor pesticides indoors.

They investigated a case concerning ordering employees to remove pipe wrap without warning them that the wrap contained asbestos.

Everything was going along perfectly fine as the cases they drew were relatively routine.

Chapter Nineteen
Taylor and Amanda at the Downstairs Bar

Taylor and Amanda went downstairs to the bar.

Amanda started, "You've been so great as a partner. There are so many things about the job that I was never taught in school or in any of the training programs. I feel so bad asking you about things that I should already know."

Taylor said, "There are so many things about environmental law which have little to do with legal training or with the environment. We learn that a company cannot dump toxic waste into lakes, rivers, and certain disposal facilities or release toxic substances into the air. We learn the legal consequences, but we do not learn some of the basics, such how violations are reported and why image is so important to the companies.

Amanda replied, "I agree."

Taylor went on, "As to reporting, it is pretty simple. You can call the environmental agency hot line on its 800 number 24 hours a day, you can call Crime Stoppers on its 800 number, or you can fill out the on-line form, which can be done anonymously.

"The California Labor Code has a whistleblower law which protects an employee from retaliation if he or she should report a violation by his or her employer.

"It's really the image question that I find most intriguing. These companies go to great lengths to cover up or minimize their environmental violations. They make crazy settlements. They will throw their entire lower management to the wolves while aggressively protecting their upper management and especially their CEO.

"Here is my brief opinion as to why this happens. Most companies are organized as corporations. A corporation is a business entity that issues stock, and the percentage of stock owned by a stockholder represents his or her percentage ownership of the business.

"There are basically two types of corporations, small and large. A small corporation is organized similar to a large corporation with articles of incorporation, bylaws, and stock. However, the two are probably taxed differently. Generally speaking, the profit made by a small corporation is included on the personal income tax return of the shareholder and is taxed to him at his personal income tax rate. This is known as a Subchapter S corporation.

"With a large corporation, on the other hand, the profit made by the corporation is treated as income to the corporation and is taxed to the corporation at the corporate tax rate. This is why the recent corporate tax cut really only helped large corporations. Only the tax at the corporate level was cut, and only large corporations tend to have this type of tax to pay. A large corporation is organized as a Subchapter C corporation.

"When a large corporation wants to raise money, after its financial track record is considered, it may apply for permission to sell stock to the public. This is called 'going public.'

"When a large corporation first sells stock to the public, it is known as an Initial Public Offering, or IPO. Corporations typically work with underwriters and investment bankers to determine the value of the stock that it will offer in its IPO.

"Though the primary objective of the IPO is to raise money for the company, founders and insiders are often able to buy stock before the rest of the public at a price lower than the IPO price. The up side is that the pre-IPO investors will own the stock at a very low price and will be able to sell it at a greater profit than someone who paid the full price. The down side is that if the IPO does not take place, the pre-IPO shares may become worthless.

"In other words, founders and insiders are able to take advantage of pre-IPO shares which are not available to the public."

Amanda jumped in, "How is that fair? Doesn't this just perpetuate the rich getting richer mentality?"

Taylor continued, "Yes it does. Lately, some non-insiders have been allowed to participate in IPOs in a limited way, but it would be my guess that they would only be allowed to participate in very risky ventures.

"Also, insiders are usually subject to a lock-up period of three to 24 months. This means that they cannot sell their stock for a stated period of time. The purpose of the lock-up is to keep the insiders from dumping their stock in the open market immediately after the stock becomes saleable. The theory is that this is more-fair to the general public. Insiders often invest in IPOs to cash out their investment in the company by selling their shares in the open market once selling is allowed.

"The money generated by an IPO goes to the company to pay for the company's business operations. After the IPO, however, the stock becomes listed on an exchange. After that, when the stock is sold, the proceeds go to the owner of the stock rather than to the company.

"The pre-IPO buyers make their profit on the difference between the pre-IPO price and the price paid by a buyer in the open market. The IPO buyers make their profit on the difference between the IPO price and the price paid by a buyer in the open market. Buyers in the secondary market make their profit on the difference between the price they paid for the stock after it became listed on an exchange and the price for which they sold the stock in the open market.

"While underwriters and investment bankers may have determined a value for the IPO shares, the value of the shares in the secondary market is much more fluid.

"The value of shares in the secondary market becomes the amount that someone is willing to pay for the shares at any given time. In other words, the value is set by the marketplace.

"Stock brokers, traders, and pundits of all types have tried many formulas to determine the potential value of a share of stock in the secondary market prior to the value being determined by the market. Thousands of books, blogs, websites, TV shows, radio programs, etc. have been devoted to this subject.

"So far no one seems to have a handle on it. No one has been completely successful in determining whether the value of a share of stock will go up or down. Some people use the price/earnings ratio. Some people consider an increase in quarterly or annual earnings. Some people consider various ratios among assets, cash, outstanding shares, etc.

"Over the years, some have argued that the media manipulates the prices through press releases.

"The only thing upon which everyone seems to agree is that the value of a share of stock in the secondary has little, if nothing, to do with the financial strength, record, or prospects of the underlying company, except emotionally.

"Now we reach the question as to why the reputation of the CEO is considered so important to protect. The CEO of a large public company represents the face of the corporation. A company with a dynamic and successful CEO is viewed as a dynamic and successful company. As a dynamic and successful company, the share price of that company is more likely to increase, or to at least to not go down.

"Conversely, if the CEO is charged or convicted of a crime or commits some other bad act, as his prestige lowers, so too might the share price.

"Because the share price is subject to going up or down whether the company is financially successful or not, the perception of the CEO may affect the share price as much or more than the company's actual business record. This is why the large public corporations are so scrupulous about the reputation of their CEOs."

Amanda said, "Now I understand why the large companies are so afraid of charges against their CEOs."

Amanda then asked, "Would the dumping or releasing of toxic chemicals be much less costly for the company if it was done illegally rather than legally. Wouldn't one of the motivations to illegally dump be to save money."

Taylor replied, "That is very true. I think at one point it would be very interesting to see how much is saved by illegally dumping and to see how those savings affect the bottom line of a big operation.

"It would seem to me to be quite risky to illegally dump if only a small amount of money is saved, seeing that the consequences are so great and are becoming more-great as time goes on.

"In the past, it used to be said that it was cheaper to dump illegally and pay the fines than to dump legally. At that time, criminal sanctions were not widely used, and if they were, the companies had no problem blaming their rank and file employees while shielding their upper management, officers, and directors.

"I don't know if we will ever be able to get into the real books of a large public corporation to find out whether or not illegal dumping makes actual economic sense."

Taylor went on, "Another point of interest is that a CEO and the other directors are not required to own a single share of stock in the company on whose Board they sit. They are on the board just to run the company."

Amanda asked, "I've always heard that rich people pay less income tax than poor people. Is that true?"

Taylor replied, "It may very well be the case that rich people pay less tax in proportion to their income than many other people, even though it is often noted that rich people may pay most of the income tax collected."

Taylor continued, "So long as unrealized capital gains are not taxed, this will remain the case. For example, if an investor owns shares of stock in a company for which he paid $50.00, if the stock goes to $100.00, until the stock is sold, he has an unrealized capital gain of $50.00. This unrealized capital gain would not be taxed in the year it is earned. It will not be taxed until the year that the stock is sold at a profit. In fact, this unrealized gain would not even be included on the income tax return of the shareholder. Even though the unrealized gain is not taxed until the shares are sold, such gain would still increase the net worth of the shareholder.

"If, on the other hand, someone earns $50.00 at his job, an activity which should be encouraged, his net worth would be increased by the same $50.00. However, he has to pay tax on this $50.00 right now in the year that it was earned. It cannot be put off. Further, the profit on his income will be taxed as ordinary income for which the tax rates are higher than capital gains rates.

"Yes, the investor will have to pay income tax when he sells. However, he may decline to sell and pay no tax, or he may sell at capital gains rates, and pay less tax. The wage earner has no choice. He has to pay the tax right now, and he has to pay at ordinary income tax rates on both his federal and state returns, which is greater than the capital gains rate.

"To take it a step further, the investor does not have to sell and pay income tax at all to access the profits in his portfolio.

"In a recent article I read, the writer said that if you have a large amount of money in your portfolio, either through your own investing or from stock you received in an IPO, you can get your money out of the portfolio without selling any of your positions and without paying income tax.

"This is done with a portfolio line of credit. You borrow against the assets in your portfolio without selling any of your stock. The proceeds of a loan are not income, and no tax is owed.

"Rich people can invest in pre-IPO shares, can do some legal insider trading of the shares in their own companies, and can hold other appreciated stock in their portfolios. This gives them unrealized capital gains which are not taxed so long as they are left in the portfolio and not sold. If sold, the rich person is taxed at capital gains rates rather than ordinary income tax rates. If not sold, the rich person can access the money by borrowing against the portfolio, and the proceeds of the loan are not taxed at all.

"Each year, a rich person can take from his or her portfolio just as much money as he or she needs to pay his or her tax-deductible expenses. He or she may write off that amount legitimately and owe no tax on it. If he needs more money, he can borrow against his portfolio, and pay no tax on the proceeds of a loan, thereby paying no tax at all. Pretty crazy.

"The IRS throws a few bones to the semi-rich. They can have IRAs, 401Ks, and Pension Plans which allow contributions to these accounts to be deducted from income in the year made and permits the money in the account to grow tax deferred. When the money is taken out of the account after retirement, the account owner will receive back his contributions tax free, but he will have to pay tax on the growth in value of his contributions at ordinary income tax rates, which are higher than capital gains rates.

"The Roth IRA and Roth 401K do not allow one to deduct one's present contributions from his present income. However, when the money is taken out after retirement, he receives back both his contributions and the growth in value of his contributions tax free.

"Municipal bonds pay tax-exempt interest. Life insurance allows money in the policy to grow tax free, and the payouts are typically free of income tax to the beneficiaries."

Taylor concluded, "Just some food for thought."

Amanda said, "This has really been fun, and informative. It's so nice to get together and catch up. I really enjoy having someone to talk to about important things. There is so much small talk in my life. Maybe I need to develop some more meaningful friendships."

Taylor replied, "That can never be a bad idea."

Chapter Twenty
Rick's Third Guest Lecture

Rick's second lecture ended during the second administration of Thomas Jefferson which ran from 1800 to 1804. During this time, the entire country was tainted with the death of Alexander Hamilton which was the result of a then legal duel with Aaron Burr.

"During Jefferson's second administration, England and France vied for trade supremacy. America came into more direct conflict with England.

"In 1808, James Madison was elected President. The Embargo Act was repealed. It was replaced by the Nonintercourse Act which provided that America would resume trade with England or France if either resumed trade with it.

"Notwithstanding the Nonintercourse Act, America continued to trade with the belligerents. Napoleon offered to restore trade with America if England would revoke its Orders of Council. Though the Orders of Council were repealed, two days later America declared war against England.

"Pressure for war was strongest in the south and west. Frontiersmen hoped that war would allow America to annex Canada to the union and would help quell the Indians. In 1811 and 1812, westerners sent war hawks, including Henry Clay, to Congress to press for war against England. Though the Federalists opposed, war was declared June 18, 1812.

"The election of 1812 served as a mandate on the war. Due to the vote of the five western states, Madison won over the Federalist Clinton.

"Then as now, wars are expensive. As we know, at this time, the United States depended largely on tariffs to support its operations. Tariffs, excise taxes, and another stamp act proved inadequate to support the war effort causing the federal government to rely on borrowing. Further the wealthiest segment of the population located in New England opposed the war and contributed little to the effort.

"The military campaigns against Canada did not go well. With Napoleon defeated in Europe in 1814, England planned a three-front attack.

"Firstly, it attempted to isolate New England. Secondly, it attacked Washington D.C. burning government buildings. Thirdly, it attacked New Orleans. Andrew Jackson defeated the English in the Battle of New Orleans which made Jackson the hero of the west and caused England to retreat. Jackson also caused the Indians to secede their best lands to the United States.

"At the Hartford Convention, New England passed a resolution stating that any State had the right to oppose an act of Congress believed to violate the Constitution. This became known as the doctrine of states' rights.

"The war ended with the Treaty of Ghent in 1814 which provided for the mutual restoration of all conquests with no mention of the interpretation of maritime law or other issues for which the United States had gone to war.

"Though technically the United States lost the war, it benefited from the defeat leveled against the Indians and from an amicable settlement of differences with England.

"The most significant benefit, however, was that the United States was no longer considered a third-rate power. This greatly lessened the temptation of other countries to meddle in American affairs and allowed America a long period of uninterrupted development."

Rick thanked his audience and let it know that the next lecture would start after the War of 1812.

Chapter Twenty-One
Paul Sinclair

Paul Sinclair was the CEO of Allied Chemical, and he had all of the trappings of his position. He graduated from Stanford with a business degree. Through family connections, he was hired for a management track position in the company. In other words, he took the path of the most entitled which often leads to the upper reaches of very large public companies.

To digress for just a minute allow me to say that I personally do not begrudge the founder of a company from eventually getting to the top and making the big money. Often times founders take huge risks. They often take an idea and start a business in their garage or at the proverbial kitchen table. Over many years, they grow the seeds of the business into a national or multi-national company which rewards them handsomely.

Even under the best circumstances, often, by the time the founder starts to realize real money, he is too old to enjoy it. This allows the company to be left to his heirs, who step into a position of untold wealth and power without the hard work or any work for that matter. In many cases, depending upon the size of the enterprise, the entire extended family of the founder never has to work.

Sometimes, the founders and other insiders make their money selling stock in the company they found, obtaining shares at their pre-IPO prices, and then holding those shares and becoming the beneficiaries of unrealized capital gains. They can pay themselves a small salary upon which they pay little tax as their salaries are used primarily for their tax-deductible expenses. If they need more money, they can borrow against their stock positions and pay no tax, as the proceeds of a loan are not taxable.

I personally am more offended by the rich kids whose parents have enough to get them into a great school and into a position in a large company, than I am by the efforts of a founder.

Founders often have to do without for many years while building their companies. They may have to invest their entire net worth as well as money advanced from credit cards or borrowed from relatives or hard money lenders. They run an enormous risk. The business could fail, and they would be out not only the time and energy expended in trying to build something but also their life savings and the money borrowed. We rarely hear about the failures. We only hear about the vast fortunes that founders make.

Rich kids, on the other hand, take no risks. They have no investment. They go to work for an established company and essentially get paid to learn. If they keep their nose to the grind stone and don't rock any boats, they might be rewarded with a position in upper management. Again, they take no risks and have no investment. A CEO is not even required to own a single share of stock in the company.

Paul Sinclair was just such a rich kid. Stanford, then Allied, then CEO of Allied. Now, at 50, he is in the prime of his corporate life.

Mr. Sinclair is married. Over the years it has been difficult for a single person to work his or her way up in the corporate world. Married men are considered more reliable and responsible. Nothing is offered here about the pool of young, attractive females, performing perfunctory roles in and around the office and what their availability might be.

One drawback for Paul was the decision of the Board to build itself a building to house its corporate offices in Lakeside, in the middle of nowhere, rather than in New York, San Francisco, or even Los Angeles.

The new corporate office tower of Allied is located in the city of Lakeside, which is in northwest Lakeside County. The plant facility, the place where things are actually made, is located in southeast Lakeside County. The Board appears to have made the decision that having the corporate headquarters in the county would humanize the operation, as it would provide jobs to residents and become the face of the company. As an ancillary benefit, housing would be cheaper for the workers.

Though Mr. Sinclair had a beautiful home in the Brentwood district of Los Angeles, the Board agreed that he should have a lavish home in the best part of Lakeside to give the appearance that he actually lived in the community, which he most certainly did not.

Mr. Sinclair knew Mr. Deaver in the Attorney General's office. He knew that Mr. Deaver had a side business of monitoring investigations of possible environmental law violations by major corporations and selling the advanced notice to various Boards. With advanced knowledge, the Boards could remain out in front of the investigations and make any adjustments necessary to keep out of serious trouble. Mr. Sinclair made such an arrangement with Mr. Deaver.

In addition, Mr. Deaver had Trey as his inside man. Trey's job was to monitor the more vigilant deputies, such as Taylor and now Amanda, to gain information about the investigations on which they were working and giving that information to Mr. Deaver to sell to Mr. Sinclair.

Taylor caused such a stir with her aggressive prosecution tactics that Mr. Deaver was forced to assign Trey to her almost full-time. He accomplished this by requiring Taylor's boss, Mr. Patterson, to accept Trey as a full-time investigator/employee and to then have him assign Trey to Taylor and Amanda on a nearly full-time basis.

Deaver's plan was to put Trey into Taylor's inner-circle. This would enable Trey to learn of her upcoming plans. Trey could then report her plans to Deaver, and Deaver could, in turn, report her plans to his stable of large corporate clients, such as Allied, to earn his retainers.

Deaver worked on the pretext that Taylor and Amanda's job was very dangerous and that Trey, as an OCI officer, was best equipped to be their protector. A pretty good cover story.

Lakeside is the largest and most affluent city in Lakeside County. It has a half-dozen or so fairly tall buildings of 10 or more floors and several buildings ranging from 6 to 9 floors.

When Allied proposed that it would build its 15-floor corporate headquarters in Lakeside, the city fathers were over-joyed. This would be a feather in their caps.

The building took two years to build, and it became a huge success for the company and the city. It has been featured on the cover of Forbes, Time Magazine, and Kiplinger as the new normal, a high-profile building representing the face of a high-profile business located in the middle of nowhere, rather than in an established downtown area such as New York, Los Angeles, or San Francisco.

The building is located at the end of one of the main streets running through downtown, near where the street reaches the edge of the desert. Tax incentives would be easy to obtain. (Probably no property taxes would be paid at all. Imagine that.)

Allied cleared a few acres of unimproved land, set the building back 65 feet from the street, and installed park-like grounds around the entire perimeter of the site. The hope was that this would impress visitors, leave plenty of room from the building to other buildings, and provide some privacy and security due to the size of the surrounding lot.

A two-way driveway apron enters from the street and connects to a 25-foot wide driveway which is asphalt with concrete curbs and gutters, similar to a finished street.

The driveway meanders to the west and expands into a wide outdoor parking area for visitors and deliveries. The entry to the underground parking garage is on the west side and is accessed by use of the driveway and part of the outdoor parking area.

The building has four levels of underground parking. The lowest level is not used for parking as the upper three levels provided adequate parking for the building's use. The 4th level is closed to the public for reasons that will become obvious.

The front of the building faces the street. It has an elaborate concrete entry patio neatly planted with local vegetation. The outdoor area is covered with a high open patio cover with a metal roof. The entire vision is almost over-whelming as one comes up to the building which extends 15 floors above.

When one enters the building, in the lobby one sees a long desk with three computer stations for receptionists. One or more of the computers is usually manned, even on the weekends. The ceiling in the lobby is two floors high creating a spectacular entry which is lavishly planted and appointed with expensive furniture, art, and furnishings.

Behind the reception desk, the ceiling drops to single story height. In this area, there is a hallway which leads to the first-floor rooms which include the security room outfitted with computers and video equipment monitoring nearly every inch of the building. Three security people man this office.

Also, behind the reception area, there are doors for eight public elevators. Two of the elevators come up from the parking floors below. From the parking area, one takes one of these two elevators to the first-floor and checks in either at reception or at an adjacent security desk. One entering the building through the front door may check in at either at reception or at an adjacent security desk. At the security desk, one is given an ID badge and sent off to the other elevators to go up to floors 2 through 15.

When someone comes into the lobby through the front door, if he intends to go up to a private office, he is directed to the security desk. If he is only dropping off a package, picking up a package, or delivering a message, this can be done at the reception desk.

At the rear of the building, there is a single service elevator. The service elevator comes from the parking garage and continues all of the way to the 15th floor office of the CEO. On each floor, the elevator door for the security elevator is located in an unfinished part of the building behind a false wall which separates the unfinished part from the finished part. Access into the security elevator may only be gained by the retinal scan of the Chief of Security or the CEO himself.

As a result, to access the service elevator, service people or movers must first visit the security desk, check in, and obtain an ID badge. They must then contact the Chief of Security to have him come to the security elevator to provide a retinal scan.

In summary, two passenger elevators run from parking levels to the lobby. The remaining six passenger elevators run from the lobby to the 15th floor penthouse. The service elevator, which may only be accessed by retinal scan, runs from the parking, all of the way up to the 15th floor with doors on each floor opening into an unfinished part of the building.

None of the several elevators runs to the roof. The only access to the roof is by a private elevator which runs from the CEO's 15th floor office directly to the roof. This private elevator may only be accessed by retinal scan.

The reason that the only access to the roof is through this private elevator is that if the building were to come under attack, only the CEO would be able to reach the roof where a helicopter would be waiting.

One may be certain that this lack of access for the general working population to the roof and rescue helicopter is not a topic of discussion at the annual spring picnic. No one, other than a few security people, know that roof access is not available to the employees generally.

As with almost every commercial building, the heating and air conditioning equipment, water heating apparatus, and other mechanical necessities are located on the roof. Sewer vents also penetrate the roof so that sewer gases may exit to the atmosphere.

The hoist-way for the private elevator extends several feet above the roof deck, high enough to accommodate a door leading onto the roof and the elevator lift equipment above the height of the door. The hoist-way appears as a small room with its own roof, extending up along the east wall of the building relatively close to the building's front wall.

The heliport is also located on the east side of the roof but in the rear corner. In short, the room for the private elevator comes up on the east side towards the front, and the heliport is located on the east side near the rear. The heliport landing area is above the level of the upper roof, as required by law for wind circulation.

The building is 100 feet wide and 150 feet deep. As such, each floor and the roof are 15,000 square feet in size. This is slightly smaller than a typical high rise in an urban setting. Most high-rise buildings have 20,000 square feet on each floor, being 100 feet wide and 200 feet deep.

However, in the middle of nowhere, the building appeared huge.

The exterior of the building is made up of dark glass panels, similar to many newer high-rise towers. Around the perimeter of the building, the panels extend above the level of the roof deck making up a parapet wall. Along the top of the parapet, there is a stainless-steel hand rail securely fastened.

As mentioned, the heliport's landing area is on the roof at the east rear corner of the building. A heliport has a touchdown and lift off area (TLOP) surrounded on four sides by the final approach and take off area (FATO). The FATO is surrounded on its four sides by the Safety Area.

The size of the final approach and take off area (FATO) is dictated by the size of the helicopter which will land there. The FATO must be 1.5 times the length of the helicopter. This means that if the helicopter is 38 feet long (which is typical), 1.5 time its length is 56 feet. The FATO would need to be 56 feet long and 56 feet wide, roughly 3,200 square feet. On a 15,000 square foot roof, the FATO appeared to be larger than 3,200 square feet, which implies that a larger helicopter could land.

The heliport's pad was elevated 2 meters (6.5 feet) above the roof which is required to allow air flow under the pad.

The offices and lab space inside of the building are quite good. However, the office of the CEO is truly spectacular.

With almost 15,000 square feet with which to work, the interior designer went a little wild. There is, of course, a huge executive office for Mr. Sinclair.

Outside of his office, there are three secretarial offices equipped with every piece of office equipment imaginable including computers, printers, scanners, shredders, recording devices, remote video screens, etc.

There is an extremely large conference room with a solid oak table and leather chairs. It is also wired to the computer equipment for power point presentations, etc.

In addition to all of the normal items that one might expect to find in a corporate office, there is also a private bedroom and a private master bathroom including a spa tub, a steam room, and a massage table. This area could only be accessed through a single hallway door which was generally closed to visitors.

All in all, Mr. Sinclair was pretty well set.

Chapter Twenty-Two
Rick's Fourth Guest Lecture and Taylor's Friday Night

Rick's Fourth Guest Lecture

Rick gave his fourth guest lecture. He reminded the class that he left off at the War of 1812. He explained that the War of 1812 was a seminal event in United States history.

"Technically, the US lost the war as its interpretation of maritime law would not prevail, and Canada would not be annexed; however, it achieved one major accomplishment which outweighed its loss. After the War of 1812, the US would no longer be considered a third-rate power on the world stage.

"After Madison won the elections of 1808 and 1812, James Monroe won in 1816. This began the Era of Good Feelings.

"The Missouri Compromise was one of the first acts of national importance which divided the country into slave and free states. Missouri entered the union as a slave State while Maine entered as a free state. There would be no slaves in States north of the 36 30 parallel.

"The Monroe Doctrine was established which stated that the Western Hemisphere would no longer be open to European colonization.

"In 1820, Monroe was re-elected. In 1824, John Quincy Adams was elected over Andrew Jackson in an election orchestrated by Henry Clay which was alleged to be unfair. The election was decided by the House of Representatives where Henry Clay was the Speaker.

"In 1828, Andrew Jackson was elected. This was seen as a reversal of the conservative trend in American politics, as Jackson was seen as the champion of the common man.

"However, as Jefferson before him, Jackson learned that the United States, with all of its sectional differences, could really only be governed by a strong centralized federal government, something that Lincoln learned the hard way when the Civil War became a reality.

"During this part of our history, tariffs were much more important than they are today. Remember, there was no income tax in those days. Revenue derived from tariffs was the primary revenue used by the federal government to run the government.

"South Carolina responded to the Tariff of 1832 with a nullification proposal. Nullification would be used to oppose actions by the federal government throughout this period.

"In 1832, Jackson was re-elected. In 1836, Martin Van Buren was elected. In 1840, William Henry Harrison was elected. He died in office and was succeeded by John Tyler.

"By the late 1830's and early 1840's labor unions were beginning to organize, and women began to press for greater rights.

"During this period, sectional differences became evident. Initially, the United States was made up primarily of farmers. As the country matured, different economic realities began to take hold in different parts of the country.

"The northeast became industrial. The south became plantation oriented. The west was populated by small farmers.

"The northeast favored high protective tariffs to protect its fledging industries. The south favored lower tariffs to permit free trade. The west remained concerned with inexpensive land.

"James Polk was elected in 1844.

"Texas was annexed in 1845. The cotton gin allowed cotton grown inland to be more easily separated from its seed. This made cotton growing in Texas viable. With a cotton crop in Texas, the issue of slavery returned to the table. The issue of slavery was transformed from a necessary evil to an economic necessity, which further polarized public opinion.

"Settlors of the United States felt that it was their Manifest Destiny to settle all of the land from the Louisiana Purchase to the Pacific Ocean.

"The Oregon Territory was annexed up to the 49th parallel. A war was fought with Mexico for California, which ended with California being annexed under the Treaty of Guadalupe Hidalgo."

Professor Miller asked whether the class thought that Manifest Destiny was a form of imperialism. He said that in his opinion it seems as if Americans felt that annexing territory to the United States, rather than subjugating the annexed people, would elevate their prospects to a position in which they too could enjoy the benefits of the American Constitution.

Apparently, the feeling that Americans had that their form of government was superior to all other forms is not much different than today.

Professor Miller continued, "By 1846, the north was trying to ban slavery in the territories. The south contended that Congress had no legal right to ban slavery from the territories as the Constitution guaranteed each citizen the protection of his property, and property included slaves.

"Zachary Taylor was elected President in 1848.

"In 1850, President Taylor asked California and New Mexico to seek admission as States. They both drew up Constitutions, and both of those Constitutions banned slavery.

"The Compromise of 1850 was drafted. Among other things, it provided that California would be admitted as a free State.

"When Taylor died, Millard Fillmore became President."

"It was hoped that the Compromise of 1850 would put an end to the slavery controversy, but that was not the case. Instead, the prosperity of the 1850s led to a reopening of the slavery question.

"Industrialization in the north provided leaders powerful enough to challenge southern plantation owners, even as expanded cotton production moved the plantation system west through Texas.

"Franklin Pierce was elected President in 1852.

"In 1854, the Kansas-Nebraska Act was passed. Under it, the relevant territories would be divided into two States, Kansas and Nebraska. Kansas would become a slave State, and Nebraska would become a free state. The Missouri compromise would be repealed. The settlers in each territory would be able to decide whether their State would become free or slave. This became known as popular sovereignty.

"James Buchanan was elected in 1856.

"Dred Scott, with his master, lived in the free State of Illinois and in the free territory of Minnesota. In State Court, it was argued that living in a free State and a free territory made Dred Scott free.

However, the State court ruled against him. The case was appealed to the Supreme Court.

"In the Supreme Court, Chief Justice Roger B. Taney ruled that the Supreme Court could not assume jurisdiction. Taney decided that Scott was not a citizen because he was a Negro, and the framers of the Constitution did not consider Negroes to be citizens. Taney ruled that Scott was still a slave, even though he had lived in a free State and a free territory. Taney also ruled that the Missouri Compromise was unconstitutional and that Congress could not prohibit slavery in the territories.

"In the 1858 Senate race, the Lincoln-Douglas Debates took place. The Freeport Doctrine was developed. Lincoln asked Douglas whether popular sovereignty was possible under the Dred Scott decision. Douglas said that it was. Douglas argued that the people of any territory could keep slavery out by refusing to enact black codes.

"In 1859, John Brown was not successful at instigating a slave uprising at Harper's Ferry.

"In the election of 1860, the Democratic Party split between Douglas and the popular sovereignty platform and Breckinridge and the Dred Scott doctrine. This left room for the Republican Party which nominated Abraham Lincoln. Lincoln ran on a popular sovereignty-type platform restricting slavery to the Sates in which it already existed, adopting protective tariffs, and passing a homestead law."

Professor Miller asked: "Was the Civil War Lincoln's choice or could moderation have delayed the war until the situation solved itself?"

Professor Miller went on, "Some argue that war could have been avoided if emotions could have been curbed. Slavery would have eventually died out on its own in the south, as it did in England.

"Others argue that war could not have been avoided because it was not about slavery at all but was about two different economic systems, industrial capitalism based on wages and staple crops based on slave labor.

"The south argued that the industrial system would eventually overcome the agricultural system. This would allow the north to make laws favorable to its own system. These laws would not be acceptable to the south where the labor system was so inefficient that only favorable legislation could keep its economy sound.

"Starting with the election of Abraham Lincoln, the southern states began to secede one by one to form the Confederate States of America. Lincoln was faced with the following very difficult question: Should he submit to a peaceful secession or should he coerce the southern States to remain in the Union with force?

"Jefferson Davis became the President of the Confederate States. Southerners believed that slavery benefitted both master and slave and that the southern economy was so inefficient that it would need favorable national legislation which would not be obtainable under a Republican president.

"Most northerners opposed coercion, believing that the southern States would return to the Union if a few concessions were made."

Professor Miller went on to tell the class that a common school of thought has been that Lincoln's decision to employ force and to engage in an armed conflict was based on the following propositions:

1. Allocating the national debt, handling fugitive slaves, and dividing the territories would never be settled peacefully.
2. Allowing secession would lead to further disunion.
3. If a disgruntled minority could leave the union whenever it chose, the south would be refusing to follow the will of the majority; this would constitute a denial of the democratic principle of majority rule.

Professor Miller told the class that guest lectures would resume next semester and would start with the outbreak of the Civil war.

Taylor's Friday Night

-----Friday, 5 p.m.

Taylor was buried in paperwork at her desk. Amanda knocked gently and opened the door. She popped her head into the office and said, "Hi, I'm going downstairs for a drink. Can you join me?"

Taylor replied, "I'm so sorry, but I'm just swamped with work."

Amanda said, "You know it's Friday and time to celebrate the end of another grueling week."

Taylor said, "I know, but I really have so much to do. And besides, Rick is out of town for a seminar for the next several days, and this would be a good time to get caught up."

"Where is he?"

"He's just in Newport Beach."

"Okay then. You know you can't work all of the time. Also, I was really hoping that we could chat and catch up. I've been so busy with Trey these last weeks that I feel as if we have not had a chance to talk, and I miss it."

"I'm sorry hun, but I really need to work."

Amanda said, "Okay. I just wanted you to know that I finally broke it off with Trey, and I was hoping we could talk about it."

Taylor replied, "Well, in my opinion at least, that is a good thing. I promise that I will make time for us to talk about it, but I just can't do it now. I am curious about it though. How did you do it?"

"I just told him that I needed something a little more serious. I'm not getting any younger, and I'm looking for something a little more permanent."

"How did he take it?"

"He seemed fine with it, which was a little unsettling."

Taylor said, "I wish it was that easy to get rid of him as our investigator. He clings to us like barnacles to a boat dock."

Amanda answered, "Isn't that true?"

Taylor responded, "He's so bad at investigating and tries so hard to minimize what we are trying to do that sometimes I wonder if he's for real. It feels almost as if he is not really investigating anything but is just trying to keep tabs on us."

Amanda responded, "We will probably never know. Anyway, it's getting late, and I'm going to go down to the bar and try to relax a little. If your schedule breaks, please come down and join me."

Taylor said, "I will, if I can. Thanks."

-----Friday, 7 p.m.

Taylor was still in her office working. She called Rick from her private cell phone.

Rick answered, "Hi, honey." He knew from caller ID that it was Taylor.

He continued, "How are you doing there?"

"Fine."

"Where are you?"

"I'm still at the office. I figured that since you were out of town, I would stay late to catch up on some paperwork."

"Don't work too hard. You need to get your rest."

"I'll rest later. I've gotten so far behind. How is your seminar? I'll bet the weather in Newport Beach is much better than it is here."

Lakeside, where Allied is located, Fairview, where Taylor's office is located, and Haven, where Rick and Taylor's home is located are all in Lakeside County. The city of Lakeside is in the western part, a little closer to Los Angeles. Fairview and Haven are in the southern part, further into the desert.

Though the corporate office building for Allied is located in the city of Lakeside, its chemical producing plant is located in the approximate center of the county between Lakeside and Fairview. It is actually a little closer to Fairview.

The city of Lakeside has some very prosperous areas, such as the area in which Mr. Sinclair's house is located. As Lakeside has a few large companies, these companies need to create the appearance that their high-level management actually lives there, so it has an expensive area. The high-level executives, such as Paul Sinclair, actually live in the best parts of Los Angeles, Orange County, San Francisco, and New York.

Outside of the city, the balance of the county is much more modest. This actually works out well for the companies as these areas provide more affordable housing for the workers, which allows them to work for less.

Newport Beach and Los Angeles are over two hours away by car with good roads in both directions.

Rick, referring to Newport Beach, continued, "The weather here is beautiful. I hope that someday I can make enough money for us to move to a place like this. I feel so bad that you have to live and work in the desert."

Taylor was quick to respond, "Don't be ridiculous. The only thing that matters is that we are together. It doesn't matter where we are. Besides, one day, between the two of us, I believe we will end up in a place that we both love."

Taylor asked, "Are you having any fun?"

Rick replies, "You know that there is no fun without you. I'm going to go over the things we covered today and get ready for TV and then bed, as usual."

"Okay honey. I'll call you tomorrow. Miss you terribly."

Taylor hung up the phone. I was already after 8 p.m.

----- Friday, 9 p.m.

Taylor dozed off for a few minutes. She was awakened by a light knock on the door on her office. Her door was just one of many doors in the AG's suite. It looked the same as all of the other doors. As a result, she was a little startled when she heard the knock.

Arousing herself, she looked at the closed door and said to the person knocking, "Hello, may I help you?"

She heard a man's voice that she did not recognize say, "I am here to see an attorney who works for the State Attorney General."

She opened the door and saw a man standing in the doorway. He appeared to be around 40 years old. He did not appear prosperous. He was wearing dirty jeans, work boots, and a tee shirt. He looked like a person who worked with his hands for a living. He moved just inside of her office but remained standing. His body language indicated that he was someone who did not mean to harm her. He was not there to rape or rob her, at least in her opinion.

While he was still standing, she replied, "And why do you need to see an attorney in the State Attorney General's office?"

He said, "I saw an article in the local newspaper that said that there is satellite office for the State Attorney General in Fairview and that this office was investigating environmental law violations."

She said, "Yes. That is true. We do investigate environmental law cases."

He said, "I have an emergency environmental violation to report."

She replied, "We do not handle emergencies. Emergencies are generally reported to the federal EPA through its 800 number or by its website."

He said, "It's after 9:00, and all of the other agencies and law enforcement offices are closed. Your office building was the only building that I could reach from the street, and your office appeared to be the only one with a person in it."

She replied, "I'm sorry, but I would need to follow the emergency protocol and report this to the federal EPA in the morning."

He said, "But that would be too late. The violation is taking place tonight. Pretty much right now."

She asked, "What is this violation?"

He said, "The big chemical company in Lakeside, Allied Chemical, is in the process of transporting liquid toxic waste for dumping in the desert. If the dumping takes place, underground water and adjacent land will become contaminated, and people might die."

She asked, "Do you know where and when this is going to happen?"

He said, "Yes. It is going to happen at Three Palms, and it will take around 30 minutes from now for the trucks to get there, and they are already on their way."

She knew about Three Palms. It was a place where illegal dumping had been suspected for years, but no one has ever been caught in the act.

Her visitor was seated by now. While he was still in her office, she tried to call the federal EPA, the State EPA, and the local Sheriff, but no one was answering at this hour. One would presume that this is just one more reason that illegal dumping takes place late at night.

"What is your name?"

"Billy."

"Well Billy, I guess we'll have to go out there and take a look ourselves."

Billy replied, "I can't do that. If they see me, I will be fired or worse, much worse. These guys, I've been told, really play rough."

Just then, out of the blue, Trey showed up at her door. He said, "I saw your light on and thought I would see what was going on."

Taylor responded, "I didn't know you were still here. I thought that you would have gone home by now."

---- Friday, 10 p.m.

Trey asked, "What's up?"

Taylor responded, "Billy here tells me that Allied Chemical is planning to illegally dump waste water in a place called Three Palms."

"When?"

Taylor replied, "Right now. Tonight."

"Oh."

Taylor said, "I'm going to run out there and take a look. It is only about 20 minutes away. I might be able to get there before Allied does."

Trey responded, "Sounds dangerous. Better let me come with you. In fact, I'll drive. We'll get there faster."

Taylor replied, "That's not necessary. I can get out there by myself."

Trey replied, "It's just too dangerous for one person. Better let me come."

Trey knew that he had only two options. He had to either go with her or keep her from going at all, preferably the later. Though he would never let on, he knew that Allied did crazy things, and he was not at all surprised to hear that they would be illegally dump at this location. At very least, he would have to accompany her for damage control.

Taylor was not thrilled about the idea of being alone with Trey in a car at 10 o'clock at night, but she did appreciate the danger.

After all, Trey was from the Office of Criminal Investigations which made him a duly sworn peace officer complete with a firearm. She thought to herself that she might actually need this type of protection.

Taylor said, "Okay. Let's get going then."

Taylor wrote Billy, Allied, and Three Palms on the first page of a small note pad on her desk, ripped off the page, and put it in her pocket. She left the note pad on her desk.

----- Friday, 10:10 p.m.

Taylor and Trey took Trey's car, a six body BMW. It would surely get them there faster than her car.

Trey inquired, "What's this all about?"

Trey was actually only testing his acting skills. He knew exactly what this was about. He had been working for Deaver who had been working for Sinclair quite a while, helping him run his illegal activities for Allied.

So far, he had done a yeoman's job of keeping the EPA at bay.

He had his methods. If a junior attorney such as Taylor got close to figuring out what Sinclair was doing, he had ways to dissuade the attorney from pursuing the investigation. If he sensed that the person was a little dishonest or had a drinking or gambling problem, he used cash bribes followed by blackmail. If he felt that the person was too honest for that, he would either report him or her for some other type of workplace violation such as sleeping with an intern or stealing supplies from the supply room to get him or her fired.

Even if there was some level of suspicion raised about a company such as Allied, trying to report it without overwhelming proof would amount to a low-level employee accusing a huge multi-national corporation of wrong-doing. A true road going nowhere.

Taylor was going to be a bigger problem. She absolutely did not care about money and lived completely within her means. This ruled out cash bribes. She had no interest in men, other than her husband, and this was well known. She was so guarded that no one at the office would even approach her.

A couple of times Trey hired a really good-looking actor to try to pick her up in the bar so he could assemble a little dirt on her. Unfortunately for the actor, the only thing he got for his trouble was being read the riot act and leaving the bar quickly, which was still much better than the beat down he would have received if he didn't leave.

She was scrupulously honest, and her honesty was near legend around the office.

Trey was hoping that somehow the tip was not good or that they decided to not dump for one reason or another. If dumping was going to be done, it was already too late to stop.

----- Friday, 10:30 p.m.

Trey and Taylor were now coming up on Three Palms. She was now ready to respond to Trey's question about what they were doing.

Taylor said, "Allied is in the business of producing and selling caustic materials to paper mills. The production of these caustic materials produces hydrogen sulfide gas. According to OSHA, hydrogen sulfide gas is an acute toxic substance which is the leading cause of death in the workplace. As such, employers are required to implement safety protocols to limit exposure to this gas.

"What peaked my interest in what Billy had to say was that there was waste water, and waste water can convey hydrogen sulfide.

"We have been following Allied and have found that a man by the name of Paul Sinclair, who is the Board Chairman, is responsible for directing production and creating disposal programs. His duties with respect to the disposal programs include the disposing of hydrogen sulfide gas, the implementation of employee safety precautions, and the purchase of employee safety equipment.

"If we do find the illegal dumping, we might also find that the transportation was made with false documents and without the required placards.

"Placards are important because they tell anyone responding to a problem with a hauler the type of material which is onboard. Otherwise, first responders have no way of knowing how dangerous the payload may be."

----- Friday 10:45 p.m.

Trey kept his composure pretty well, pretending that he did not know anything about that of which she was speaking. They were coming up on three Palms.

Trey said, "It looks like we are way too late here. Nothing to see here. We should probably turn back so we can get home at a reasonable hour."

Taylor snapped, "No. Don't do that. We are here now. We need to get out and take a look."

As they approached the dump site, they saw an abandoned building with pretty good vision of the surrounding area. They got out of the car and went into the building. From the building, they could see that three trucks bearing the name Allied Chemical on their sides were already at the dump site but had not completed their dumping.

Trey, now in complete panic-mode, said, "We have to get out of here. If we get caught, we might get shot, and they will be able to say that we were trespassing or were here to rob them."

Taylor replied, "I'm not going anywhere except closer for a better view."

With that, Taylor got into a position from which she could see the entire dumping operation. Trey, displeased, also looked at the dumping.

Trey remarked, "We really need to get out of here now."

The second truck was unloaded and the liquid was poured out into the desert.

"Not a chance. I've seen two thirds of an illegal dumping operation, and I plan on seeing the rest."

The third truck was opened, and barrels were beginning to be removed and then dumped.

As the dumping was underway, a driver standing nearby convulsed and fell to the ground. He appeared dead. The other workers were beginning to panic. The person in charge came over to have a look at the commotion.

He reached down to the neck of the man lying on the ground to feel for a pulse. Though Taylor and Trey could not hear him, he appeared to be telling the other workers that the person was dead. He ordered two of the other men to put the dead body into one of the empty barrels and to close the lid. Taylor presumed that they would look for a place to dump it.

Taylor said to Trey, "Wow, I have to call the police right now."

While holding her cellphone and looking at the dial, perhaps to get a better cell signal, she turned away from Trey; and then bang. Trey hit her across the back of the head with a night stick he was carrying. It knocked her out. When the head receives a trauma, the brain shifts and contacts the side of the skull. When the trauma is sufficient, the brain shuts down, and blood is diverted to the brain, as the brain performs so many functions that sustain life.

Stun guns only stun temporarily. Chloroform needs to be applied for several minutes continuously and then re-applied again and again. But a crack to the back of the head puts someone out right now and for a long time particularly when, as here, the person has no notice that he or she will be hit. If the person has notice, he or she might be able to move his or head away from the blow which might dampen it. That was not the case here.

Taylor knew that there was something not right about Trey, but she did not think that he was complicit with others working against her. The blow to the head proved that her thinking about Trey was very wrong.

----- Saturday, 12:30 a.m.

Trey used his encrypted phone to call Mr. Deaver.

Deaver answered, "Why are you calling me. You know that you are never to call me. Never."

Trey responded, "But I have a real emergency here, and I need to know what to do."

Deaver inquired, "What happened."

Trey responded, "Taylor received notification fairly late at night either from someone working at Allied or from someone who knew someone working at Allied that there was going to be an illegal toxic waste dump which was going to take place within 30 minutes. It was too late to call the police or the EPA, so being the pain in the ass that she is, Taylor decided to investigate the allegation herself. I could not let her go alone, or who knows what she would find and to whom she would report. Making her think that I wanted to go along as her protection detail, I went with her. I even drove. I was trying to show that I cared about her safety, which I did not.

"We went out to Three Palms, the place where the tipster told her that the dumping would take place. We hid in an abandoned building and saw three trucks belonging to Allied backing in to make their dump. The first two trucks were unloaded, and the dumping went fine. However, with the third truck, one of the drivers got exposed to the hydrogen sulfide that they were carrying. His exposure was so great that he died."

Deaver asked, "How do you know that he was dead?"

Trey said, "They loaded his limp and lifeless body into an empty barrel, closed and fastened the lid, and placed the closed barrel back on the truck to be disposed of elsewhere, I guess. I don't think that they would have put him in the barrel and sealed it if they thought that there was even a chance that he was still alive."

Deaver said, "That is really bad. Not the death, but the fact that it was witnessed. Particularly the fact that it was witnessed by someone so gung ho against environmental law breakers. The witness could not have been worse."

Trey said, "I cannot disagree with you there."

Deaver asked, "Where is Taylor now? Please don't tell me that you are so stupid that you let her walk away."

Trey said, "Of course not. I would never do anything like that. I knocked her out, put a hood over her head, bound her legs together, bound her arms to her waist, and handcuffed her to the inside of my car. The problem is that I don't know what to do with her now."

Deaver said, "I will need to call my contact at Allied and ask him. Just drive around, and I will call you back."

Deaver hung up the phone and called Mr. Sinclair on his encrypted phone.

Mr. Sinclair answered, "Why are you calling me? You know that you are never to call me under any circumstances."

Deaver replied, "We have a serious emergency. One of my guys went with one of the deputy AGs to investigate a possible illegal toxic waste dump by Allied. The tip came in when someone just showed up in the office and said that the dumping was going to take place within 30 minutes. It was so late in the day that the deputy AG could not reach the local authorities or the EPA, so she decided to take the call herself and go out to the site.

"My guy could not talk her out of it so he went with her to try to mitigate any damage she might cause if she actually saw something. When they got there, they saw three Allied trucks unloading waste water. When the third truck was being unloaded, one of the drivers was exposed to hydrogen sulfide gas. The man died. The other Allied people put him in an empty barrel and loaded him back in one of the trucks."

Sinclair responded, "So, a deputy AG witnessed one of our drivers get killed by hydrogen sulfide during an illegal dump? Please tell me that you did not just let her get away?"

Deaver stated, "No, of course not."

Sinclair asked, "So what did you do with her?"

Deaver said, "My guy knocked her out, put a hood over her head, tied her up, and put her in his car. He called me to find out what to do next."

Sinclair said, "This is bad. She's an attorney, I presume. That means she has a family who will miss her."

Deaver asked, "What should I tell my guy to do?"

Sinclair said, "For now, he should take her to the headquarters building in Lakeside. By the time they get there, it will be late enough that they can get into the parking garage go down to the fourth level, where no one parks, without being seen. I'll have the door to that level open. There's a makeshift jail cell down there where my people can put her, at least for now."

Deaver said, "Okay. What will happen after that?"

Sinclair replied, "I don't know. But I will come up with a plan."

Deaver hung up the phone and called Trey. He told Trey to take Taylor to the Allied Chemical corporate headquarters building in Lakeside and to proceed down to the fourth level of underground parking. He was to wait for further instructions.

----- Saturday, 2 a.m.

Trey drove his vehicle to the Allied headquarters. He entered the underground parking garage and wound his way down to the fourth level.

A separate gate for the fourth level was open allowing him to proceed. He passed the gate, continued down the ramp, reached the fourth level, and went around the corner to the open area which was not being used for parking.

The set up in the fourth level was unexpected and, frankly, a little ominous, even to Trey. In the parking garage, the parking area is surrounded by full height perimeter concrete walls which retain the underground earth into which the garage was built. On one side of the garage, covering several square feet, there is a large free-standing cell or cage with metal bars all around which included a barred entry door.

Inside of the cage, there is a cot for the occupant. There was evidence that various forms of torture could be carried on around the cage, as there was room for water boarding and high voltage shock.

Outside of the cage along the south wall of the parking garage, there was a white cabinet approximately three feet high and 22 inches deep. In the cabinet on the right side, there was a single bathroom-style basin. Above the cabinet on the left side, there was an upper cabinet with glass doors.

Behind the glass doors, one may see some medications including sodium pentothal and sodium thiopental. Both of these drugs are used as truth serums for interrogations. Neither has been very successful. Under their influence, though one might have reduced inhibitions, he or she is still able to lie and to even fantasize. They are not in wide governmental use but appear to be in use in this extra-legal setting.

Trey drove his car down driveway. He continued to the location near the door to the cage. Taylor was now semi-conscious.

Three security guard types pulled her from the car and carried her into the cage. Her head was still covered with the hood, and her legs and waist were still bound. One of the security guards gave her a shot, telling her it was a sedative for her own good to keep her from becoming agitated and injuring herself.

The tape binding was removed from her legs and waist. The hood was removed. She was able to see that she was in a cage in, what appeared to be, a parking garage. She did not know whether the concrete room was at ground level or was underground. Her feeling was that it was underground due to the cool temperature.

She thrashed around, but the sedative made it impossible for her to speak clearly or to move freely.

Even Trey, who did not like Taylor, felt bad for her. This kind of captivity could only mean a long period of extreme discomfort followed by death. How could she be let go after witnessing a killing, being kidnapped, and suffering imprisonment in a horrible cage cell?

Trey's only happiness was that he would be getting out of there soon. So, he thought.

Taylor was placed on the cot, which, it appeared would serve as her bed.

Taylor tried to ask what she was doing there and when she could leave. The security guard that gave her the shot told her that she would be staying in the cell as long as necessary.

From all that could be seen, there was one thing that was certain. As to the person who designed this cage and its accoutrements, this was not his first rodeo.

Chapter Twenty-Three
Rick's Saturday Morning

Rick woke up in his hotel room in Newport Beach at 6 a.m. He called Taylor. Her phone rang five times and went to voicemail.

This was most unusual. When Rick was away from home, Taylor was always up at 6 a.m. and always answers her phone as she knows it will be Rick.

When Taylor did not answer, Rick called Rosie Valdez, his next-door neighbor. Rosie answered the phone.

"Hello."

"Hi, Rosie, it's Rick from next door. Sorry to call so early. I tried to call Taylor, but she did not answer, and she always answers, particularly when I'm out of town."

Being a good person and a great neighbor rather than making a big deal about him calling so early she instead said, "No problem. I guess you're worried about her?"

"Yes."

"Let me take a look to see if her car is in your driveway."

Rosie put down the phone and went to her front window. From there, she could see the full length and width of Rick and Taylor's driveway.

"I don't see her car in the driveway, which is unusual. It's always there at this hour."

Rick replied, "Yes. It is."

Rosie responded, "Would you like me to run over and knock on the door. Maybe she had car trouble and got a ride home."

"Thanks. That would be great. I'll call you back in a few minutes."

Rosie put on a robe and slippers and ventured across the driveway to Rick's front door. He knocked on the door, but there was no answer. It appeared as if no one was home.

Rick called back.

"Was she home?"

Rosie responded, "It did not appear as if she was."

Rick said, "Thank you so much for checking. I'm not going to waste any time wondering. I'm heading back now."

Rick thought about what he would do. His first impulse was to contact Moose for help.

Moose is about as good a resource as one could have if he is in trouble or knows someone who is in trouble. He is an ex-army Ranger and has several ex-service person friends who are always willing to help, and who are similarly equipped.

For the past many years, Moose has been the President of a motorcycle club called the Motorcycle Enthusiasts of America or MEA for short. The club has meetings a couple of times a year, and its members share stories about motorcycles and their uses. He also runs a mail order business through which he sells motorcycle memorabilia imprinted with the MEA logo.

When Moose was starting out, he ran afoul of the IRS and was audited. His accountant so understated his income that the IRS was considering fraud charges. He was referred to Taylor who though young did the books for her family farm. Her family consisted of only her and her mother as her father had walked out on them when she was just 10.

Taylor was able to reconstruct Moose's books which allowed Moose to comply with the audit for a nominal amount. Moose was very appreciative. Taylor, Moose, Moose's wife, and Moose's friends all became friends.

A couple of years later, when she was 17, Taylor was babysitting a little girl by the name of Tammy Fitzgerald. Tammy was kidnapped by a notorious gangster and held captive at his mountaintop compound. It was eventually discovered that the gangster kidnapped the little girl to persuade the little girl's father to complete his obligation to build a casino project for the gangster.

With respect to the kidnapping, there was no body and no ransom demand. The police, who were either incompetent, complicit, or both allowed the case to go cold.

Taylor would not believe that Tammy was dead and set out on a one-person crusade to find her and bring her home. During her search, she met Rick who was teaching a class that she was taking at the local junior college.

Taylor and Rick suspected that Tammy was being held at the gangster's compound. While trying to get a closer look, Taylor was captured and imprisoned. This meant that both she and Tammy were being held. Rick enlisted Moose's help to rescue both of the girls. Moose and his friends stormed the compound and rescued Taylor and Tammy, and Tammy was returned to her parents.

As Tammy's father was complicit in her kidnapping, he and Tammy's mother split.

There were several criminal and civil trials. Taylor used the settlement that she received to finance her education.

Taylor went on to college and law school and began working for the California State Attorney General in Fairview. She and Rick began dating and were then engaged. She started her work with the AG first in elder abuse and then in white collar crime specializing in environmental law.

She and Rick married and bought a home in Haven. Rick continued to work for the DA, and Taylor for the AG.

When Rick was unable to reach Taylor and learned from his neighbor that her car was not in the driveway, he had a feeling that she was in trouble. Nothing specific. Just a feeling.

After hanging up with Rosie, Rick wasted no time. He checked out of his room, threw his suitcase in the car, and headed back towards Taylor's office in Fairview, rather than their home in Haven.

While driving, he would have time to plan out his next move and to call Moose.

At 6:30 a.m., he called Moose. A woman answered, "Hello, Motorcycle Enthusiasts of America, Carol speaking."

"Is Moose there?"

"Yes. May I ask who's calling?"

"This is Rick, Taylor's husband."

"Oh, hi. Let me get him."

Moose came on the line, "Hello."

"Moose, this is Rick, Taylor's husband. I think Taylor is in trouble. I was out of town but cut my trip short when I was unable to reach her this morning. She is always available at 6 in the morning. I telephoned our next-door neighbor who told me that her car was not in the driveway. I dropped everything, and I am heading back."

Moose replied, "Could it be something else."

"I don't think so."

Moose continued, "It can't be that she is having an affair. She doesn't even like men, except for you. Unless someone snuck up on her, she could hold her own with any three guys, specially the kind of guys she would run into at her office or in a bar. I think your instincts are probably right. She is probably in some kind of trouble. How long will it take you to get back, and what is your plan?"

"I should be back by no later than 8:30. My plan is to go to her office to see if her car is there. If her car is there, then I will know that she was either taken by force or accepted a ride from someone. If she accepted a ride, it has to be with someone she knows well. She is not the kind of person who accepts rides from just anyone."

"What is the address of the place?"

"1502 Avenue C, Fairview."

"I'll see you there at 8:30."

Rick hung up the phone and put his foot on the gas. Being so early on a Saturday, the roads were pretty clear. He could be early.

Rick arrived at Taylor's office building before Moose. He parked his car and walked up to the front door. The door was locked. It was Saturday.

A metal door was brought down over the entrance to the parking garage. On the weekends access to the parking garage was not available. He would have to try something else.

He went back to the front door. The doors were glass. One could look through the doors and see clearly into the lobby.

Rick saw a middle-aged Latin man pushing a grey plastic trash can on a cart along with brooms, mops, buckets, and other cleaning implements and supplies. He knocked on the glass door trying to get the gentleman's attention. When the man looked over, Rick motioned for him to come to the door.

The man came over. They were now standing approximately six inches apart from one another separated only by the glass pane of the door.

Rick said in a loud voice, "Could you please open the door? I need to get inside to look in the parking garage and an office."

The man replied, "I am not allowed to do that. If I let you in, I will lose my job."

Rick said, "I think that my wife is in trouble, and I need to get in to find out."

The man replied, "Who is your wife?"

Rick replies, "She works here in the Attorney General's Office."

The man asked, "What is her name?"

Rick responded, "Taylor Shaw."

The man replied, "Oh Miss Shaw. I know her. She is the pretty one who is so nice."

"Yes, that would be she."

The man continued, "She is the only one in this whole place who is kind and who treats us like people."

Rick anxious but trying to be respectful responded, "Yes. She is a truly wonderful person. But I'm afraid that she is in trouble, and I need to get in to see."

The man resisted, "Maybe you could call Miss Amanda. She is the young one that your wife is teaching."

Rick thought to himself that he did not know that Taylor was also tasked with teaching the beginning lawyers. He said, "Is she teaching her the law?"

The man replied, "Oh no senior, much more important than that. She is teaching her how to be a good person. A far more important lesson."

Rick replied, "That is wonderful, but I still need to get into the building because though my wife speaks of a young lawyer by the name of Amanda, I do not know how to reach her. If she works with my wife, she too could be in trouble."

The man finally relented. He opened the door with a key just above floor level. Rick came into the lobby.

Rick said, "Thank you so much sir. I need to see if my wife's car is here. Do you know where she parks?"

"Of course, senior. She parks on P2 near the back. Sometimes if she is leaving late, me or one of my sons will watch to make sure that she gets to her car safely. You cannot be too careful in an underground parking lot."

Just then, Moose, Bart, Lester, and a younger, not quite as robust fellow showed up at the front door. Rick was thinking to himself that he had never been so happy to see four people as he was right then.

Moose said, "Hi Rick. I see that you have gotten in. Knocking the broom out of Bart's hand. He loves to pick locks. What's your plan?"

"I have just met this nice fellow. He knows Taylor. After explaining that she might be in trouble, he was kind enough to let me in. I thought I would see if her car was here. He was just going to show me where she parks. I thought that after that we might get a look in her office to see if there is anything there."

Moose said to my Latin friend, "And sir, may I know your name?"

"Jorge Luis."

"Thank you."

The six of them entered the elevator. Jorge pressed P2. The door opened on P2, and they all exited the cab. Jorge looked across the garage towards the rear.

"There it is. Her car is parked in her regular spot."

Rick said, "This means that she was either taken in another vehicle or she went with someone voluntarily in his or her vehicle."

They then asked Jorge to take them to her office.

They entered the elevator. Jorge pressed 4. They reached the 4th floor and exited into the hallway. They turned left and went down to the end of the hall. They entered a suite. The suite was at the end of the hall which implied that it probably had several offices. The entry door was a double door. On the right-hand door, there was a placard which read, "The Office of the Attorney General of the State of California."

They entered the private reception area for the suite. No one was there as it was Saturday, and the office was closed.

Fortunately, Jorge had keys to all of the offices. He took them to Taylor's private office within the suite and let them in.

It was a typical government lawyer's office. It had a large wooden desk. Not fancy. There was a chair behind the desk, and two chairs for visitors in front of the deck. There was a computer on the return. Below the computer, there was a printer. Interestingly enough, Rick had never been to Taylor's office. The need never presented itself. But here he was now.

There were a couple of framed prints of landscapes on the wall. There were two file cabinets.

Rick said, "The first thing I think we should do is to try to contact Amanda. She might have some information. At least she will know what types of cases Taylor was working on."

Moose motioned to the fourth man, the man whose name Rick did not know, to look at the computer. The man's name was Dave

Wilson, and, it turns out, he was a computer specialist. The right guy to have along.

Moose said, "Dave, do you think you can get any info from the computer?"

Dave replied, "Let me give it a try."

Dave worked on the computer while Rick looked around the office for any handwritten notes or correspondence.

Dave asked, "What are we looking for?"

"Amanda's full name, telephone number, and address would be good."

Dave's fingers flew across the keyboard. Various screens came up, overlapped with one another, then disappearing when not needed.

"I think I have something here."

Dave pulled up a screen. At the top it said "Contact Information for Office Personnel."

The names were in alphabetical order. Following the list down, he saw the name "Amanda Warren" with her phone number and address.

Dave said that this must be she, as she was the only "Amanda" on the list.

Rick said, "I think that I will just call her. It would save a great deal of time compared to driving over there."

Moose added, "Good idea."

Rick took the number from Dave and dialed Amanda on his cellphone. A woman answered.

"Hi, this is Rick Miller. I know that we have never actually met, but I am Taylor's husband."

Amanda replied, "If this is that Rick Miller, Taylor speaks of you often."

Rick said, "Allow me to tell you that I am a little worried about Taylor. I called her this morning at 6 a.m., and she did not answer, which is unusual. I called our next-door neighbor who told me that her car was not in the driveway. I was away at a seminar, but when I couldn't reach her, I drove back to her office immediately. I've heard that your office is also on this floor but down the hall."

Amanda replied, "Why did you go to our office. Why not home?"

Rick said, "Our next-door neighbor already told me that Taylor's car was not in the driveway. I figured I would come to the office to see if it was here. If still here, I would know that she was either taken by force or that she voluntarily went with someone in his or her car. I thought this might narrow down the number of people who might know her whereabouts."

Amanda said, "I feel a little funny talking to you about her as I have no way of knowing that you are who you say you are."

Rick said, "Fair enough. Let's try facetime."

Rick set his cellphone and held the screen in front of his face so it would be seen on Amanda's phone.

Amanda saw the image and said, "You are definitely the same person in the photo on her desk."

Rick looked over at her desk and saw the photo of the two of them on their honeymoon.

Rick said, "Good. As I said, I came to her office to see if her car was here. It is not. I spoke with her around 6:30 last night. She probably left the office after that time. Did you see her after 6:30?"

Amanda replied, "No. I went downstairs, and when she did not join me, I went home."

Rick asked, "Was there anyone else still in the suite around that time?"

Amanda answered, "Yes, Trey was still there."

Rick asked, "Would she leave with Trey?"

Amanda answered, "She would definitely not leave with Trey for any social reason. She really didn't like him and counseled me to stay away from him. But she might go with him voluntarily for a business reason."

Rick asked, "What do you mean by a business reason?"

Amanda answered, "Trey is with OCI. A few weeks ago, he was assigned to me and Taylor to provide us with protection during our investigations into environmental crimes. I guess the brass thought that environmental investigations into big companies could get dangerous, as big companies do not like governmental agencies investigating their business, which was not always completely legal."

Rick asked, "Did he ever get fresh with Taylor?"

Amanda answered, "I think you know the answer to that question. If he ever did get fresh with her, she would probably have given him a beatdown."

Rick replied, "Now I know that we are talking about the same person."

Rick continued, "Were you working on any investigations which might have been undertaken after 6:30 last night?"

Amanda replied, "No. Not that I am aware of."

Rick asked, "Could such an investigation come into the office after 6:30?"

Amanda replied, "I guess that would be possible. The State EPA does not typically get involved in emergencies. Emergencies are generally referred to the federal EPA's 800 number or to the local authorities. However, one can't rule out the possibility that an emergency could come into the office after hours, particularly if it concerned a violation which was going to take place that night. Presuming that the federal EPA and the local authorities were not reachable, knowing her, she might take up such the investigation herself, and she might even allow Trey to tag along for protection, as that was his job."

Rick said, "If there is even the possibility that there may have been an after-hours violation, I would feel better if I sent a guy to your place to keep an eye on you. If something Taylor learned put her in danger, it might also put you in danger. Text me your address, and I will send someone over there. His name is Bart. You will know him when you see him. He's an ex-army Ranger and is around 70."

Amanda replied, "I don't think that will be necessary, but it's okay with me."

Rick replied, "Maybe not, but if you do need help, he will be the perfect person for the job. That I guarantee."

Amanda texted her address, and Bart was dispatched to her place.

Rick then turned to Jorge Luis and asked, "Do you know this Trey person? Is he okay?"

Jorge responded, "El es muy mala persona. He's a bad dude. He's so rude and thinks he is such a big shot. He has not been very nice to Amanda. Taylor is too smart to fall for his tricks."

Rick looked at Moose and said, "We need to find out what kind of car he has. If we find the car, we will probably find him. We will need his address and phone number also."

Jorge said, "He drives a fancy BMW 6 body. A beautiful car."

Dave hit the computer. He found Trey's address and phone number.

Rick said to Jorge, "Can you say now that your service for the rest of the weekend is complete. I think it would be better if you and your family leave now and get away from the building. I know one thing for certain, whoever is in charge of whatever it is that Taylor may be mixed up in will certainly be sending someone here to search her office, and these guys will be dangerous. You and your family have been so helpful that I would not want to see any of you get hurt."

Jorge replied, "I am not quite finished, but if you think it would be better, I will pack up and leave now."

Rick replied, "Good."

Rick looked around the room for a last time.

Moose asked, "What are you looking for?"

Rick replied, "Anything that looks out of place. Anything that looks like the normal procedures that Taylor might otherwise follow were not followed because she was in a hurry to get out of here. And I believe that this is it."

Rick looked at all of the papers and files neatly stacked around the office. He looked at the computer. Dave had done a search of all of the documents which were produced within the past 36 hours and did not find anything about a late-night emergency anywhere.

Rick found a small yellow legal pad which appeared to be used for handwritten notes. It just looked a little out of place. The top page appeared to be blank, but Rick could see indentations in the form of letters on the page. He recognized the handwriting as Taylor's. He thought that he could make out the words "Billy" and "Three Palms." There was another word which appeared to begin with the letter "A," but he could not make it out.

Rick said to Moose, "This looks like a last-minute note that Taylor may have written to herself."

He looked at Jorge and asked, "Does the name 'Billy' or the place 'Three Palms' mean anything to you?"

Jorge replied, "The name 'Billy' does not mean anything. But there is a place called 'Three Palms.' It is way out in the middle of the desert. No one goes out there, ever."

Dave was still at the computer. He said, "I've been through the employment records for the office, and I have found no one named 'Billy,' 'William,' 'Will,' 'Bill,' or any name similar to these names working here. This is a very small office, and the search would be very complete."

Rick said, "That actually makes sense. It would be much more likely that someone coming here to report an environmental crime would not be working here. It would be much more likely that he would be working at the place committing the crime."

Moose asked, "What next?"

Rick asked Jorge, "How far is Three Palms?"

Jorge replied, "20 or 30 minutes, depending on how fast your car is."

Rick looked at Moose and said, "Guess we're going to Three Palms."

Chapter Twenty-Four
Rick's Saturday Mid-Day

Rick, Moose, Lester, and Dave drove to Three Palms. It was way out in the desert, but there was no traffic. Bart went to Amanda's.

They saw the same abandoned building that Taylor saw which looked down to a low area which appeared to be a dry lake bed. They drove down to the low area. It was difficult to determine whether it was a dry lake bed left over from some ancient spring or was a dry area caused by the dumping of liquid waste over the dry land. They got out of the car to inspect.

The first thing that struck all of them was the smell. It smelled like rotten eggs.

Moose asked, "What the heck is that smell? It smells like rotten eggs."

Rick answered, "If I am not mistaken, that would be hydrogen sulfide."

Moose asked, "What is hydrogen sulfide?"

Rick explained, "Drainage pipes tend to have slime buildup on their inside walls. When the pipes are running flat, waste water does not flow freely down the line, and the liquid stagnates creating a septic condition.

"With a septic condition, the bacteria use all of the available oxygen while decomposing organic matter for energy. Drain pipes with low flow encourage bacteria growth. The bacteria in the slime layer reduces sulfur compounds to sulfides.

"Under septic conditions, sulfides cannot be oxidized. Therefore, they combine with hydrogen to produce hydrogen sulfide gas, creating the rotten egg smell.

"Taylor was telling me about a case where a chemical company illegally dumped wastewater containing hydrogen sulfide which caused the death of two of the truck drivers transporting it. The

President of the company was sentenced to 12 months in federal prison and ordered to pay a fine of $5,000.

"Though to us this might seem like a ridiculously light sentence, to a guy who has been CEO of a large company and who is used to living the good life with expensive homes, cars, country clubs, jets, vacation homes, etc., it might seem like the end of the world. To him, covering up a death might be worth doing, particularly if the deceased person is a nobody, or nobody to him.

"Taylor was asking me whether, depending on the facts, I thought that the criminal part of the violation could be charged as second-degree murder rather than involuntary manslaughter. Second degree murder carries penalties which are much more stringent than one year."

Moose said, "I see your point. If Taylor saw something like that go down, if the perp found out, she would be in real danger. What next?"

Rick replied, "I'm going to have a look around. With all of the commotion of the dumping and someone dying, maybe someone made a mistake and left something which could help identify them."

Rick began searching the area. Over the years, he had been at several crime scenes for his job with the DA and watched how the forensic people investigated. Nothing was too small or insignificant. These were detail people. The big picture was not their thing. They collected the most minute pieces of evidence.

They had the luxury of being able to collect and take items back to a lab or to send items to a specialist.

For example, if insects were collected, they could be sent to an entomologist, and a scientific determination could be made as to which substances or liquids would attract those particular insects. The life span or gestation period of an insect would give clues as to when crimes may have been committed.

If certain plant or other organic material not typically associated with a particular area was found, that could be an indication that the material was brought in from somewhere else, and that location could be determined.

Rick looked along the perimeter of the area where it appeared as if the dumping took place. Tire treads from three large semis could be seen terminating before they reached the softer earth. This would imply that the vehicles backed into this area, stopped, unloaded their cargo, and poured the illegal liquid or spread the illegal substance they were carrying onto or over the ground.

Rick, Moose, and Lester looked along the edge of the dump site for anything. Rick found a mutilated and discarded piece of paper which looked as if it might have been a work order from a legitimate job that fell out of the truck and was not picked up.

Rick asked Moose, "Wasn't there a diner a few miles up the road? I'm sure that many trucks stop there and that the waitstaff knows the comings and goings of many of the drivers. I think that we should go to the diner and see if they know anything."

Moose, Lester, and Dave agreed. They were hungry anyway. They got into Rick's Suburban and headed up the road.

Rick spotted a lone building which appeared as if it might be the diner for which they were looking. It had a neon sign that said "Molly's Diner." It was a one-story stucco box with a flat roof with parking around the building. Rick parked in the lot on the south side. They all went inside.

It was the type of diner that one would expect to see in the 1960s or 70s. There was a long counter with a plastic-like top bound with a metal edge. There were fixed stools on an elevated step below the over-hanging counter-top. There were six tuck and roll vinyl booths under the windows along the front and east sides.

They decided to take a booth.

A nice-looking middle age lady dressed in her waitress attire came over to the booth and asked, "What can I get you boys?"

Moose and Lester each ordered a cheeseburger, fries, and a Coke. Dave and Rick each ordered a grilled chicken sandwich, a side salad, and ice tea.

After she finished taking the order, Rick asked, "Have you seen any large trucks come by here in the past few hours?"

She replied, "Honey, I see trucks come by here all day and all night, every day."

Rick went on, "There may have been three of them together headed towards Three Palms."

She replies, "Oh, I've heard about that place. I stay away from everything to do with it. Not only is talking about that place bad for business, it can also be seriously bad for your health, if you know what I mean."

Rick understood her plight, but he was starting to get a little desperate. So far, they had driven all of the way out to Three Palms, and they still did not have any idea where Taylor might be.

He did know, however, that whoever had Taylor would keep her alive only long enough to find out what she knows and who else knows what she knows. After that, they would have no use for her, and because of her threat to their enterprise, they would have to dispose of her, in a permanent way. Their alternative would be to try to discredit her, and they all knew that that would never work. Her reputation for veracity, and accuracy, were legend. They would have no alternative but to kill her.

Rick knew a few investigative tricks from his work with the DA. He could take tire impressions; he could check for DNA or fingerprints from some of the surfaces; he could check shoe sizes and impressions from the soft earth. He could take insect samples, soil samples, and collect much additional evidence to be sent to a lab.

Unfortunately, all of these things would be useless as they would take time, and time was the one thing that he did not have. All of the normal methods of investigation were out the window.

All they had left was to coerce the information from someone who knows something, a practice Rick did not relish.

He pressed the waitress again, "I'm really sorry to press, but my wife is in danger, and we really need the information about any trucks which may have been heading for Three Palms. If we cannot get this information right now, it might be too late to save her. Please tell us if you have seen any caravans of three large semi-trucks?"

She had a look of painful understanding but still replied only reluctantly, "There were a few groups of truck caravans that came through here. There are not many businesses in the area large enough to support a three-truck convoy. There's United Trucking, Swift Transfer, Alsco, Allied Chemical, Reliable Van and Storage, Southwest Chemical, Petrol Chemical, and a couple of others."

"We found this tiny piece of paper at Three Palms. Do you remember anyone in a three-truck caravan leaving anything like this in the restaurant?"

She replied, "No, but it is possible none of the trucks for which you are looking stopped here."

She asked to look at that the paper again.

She replied, "This looks like a standard shipping order. I have seen hundreds of these things over the years. It could come from any one of the companies. But I do think that a shipping order would come from a company that was shipping something it made or a product made by someone else. Furniture deliveries usually include an inventory of the items shipped. But this won't help you much anyway because if the trucks were headed to Three Palms, there would be no written order anyway."

(It appears as if she knew more about what went on at Three Palms then she let on.)

Rick concluded, "Thank you for all of your help."

They paid the check, left a generous tip, and moved to Rick's car.

Rick then said to the collected group, "We need to work not only harder, but much smarter than we have been. The waitress gave us a list of companies that may have had trucks in the area. We need to get to google and see what companies have facilities in this area that might use large trucks.

"This is not a street crime. When criminals commit a street crime, they go out and steal a car and commit their crime. After the crime is done, the stolen car is dumped or burned.

"We are looking for a company with toxic waste to dump. It cannot go out and steal a semi to commit that crime. It has to use a vehicle that it already owns.

"These are large, public companies. A large, public company has to present a high-profile face to the public. Presenting a high-profile face is one of the several ways it has to communicate its impressive success, which, in turn, bolsters its stock price.

"Large, public companies use the sides of their trucks as veritable billboards advertising their success.

"If we look over our list, we will be able to rule out some of the companies. The presence of hydrogen sulfide, that smell we all noticed, would more likely indicate chemical waste.

"United and Reliable generally carry furniture. Swift typically carries food. Alsco is a commercial laundry and typically carries laundry equipment and, sometimes, clothing.

"This leaves Allied, Southwest, and Petrol. They are all chemical companies and, according to everything Taylor told me, a chemical company is the type of company which might be more likely to carry hydrogen sulfide which produces the odor we smelled at the site, and would more likely be the type of company for which we are looking."

Rick continued, "It would be so great if we had access to traffic cameras."

He concluded, "I think we should go back to Amanda's house, hook up with her and Bart, and make a plan. As we all know, they are going to keep Taylor alive only long enough to find out what she knows, so we need to move quickly."

———

Unknown to Rick and Moose by the time they left the diner and headed back towards Amanda's, the offices of Taylor and Amanda had been tossed, and their computers taken.

Fortunately, Rick removed any scrap of paper, including the note pad, which could have anything to do with Three Palms, and Dave had scrubbed the computers clean, even though they had no information of use on them.

Chapter Twenty-Five
Rick's Saturday Afternoon

As Rick, Moose, Lester, and Dave headed back towards Amanda's house, Moose asked: "Should we go to the police station?"

Rick replied, "That is probably a good idea, though I do not think that it will achieve anything. But who knows, maybe they have a traffic camera out on the route to Three Palms?"

Moose said, "I agree that it will not achieve anything, but it might give us some cover later. Also, asking about traffic cameras cannot hurt."

As it was on the way to Amanda's anyway, Rick said, "Okay then."

They drove into downtown Fairview and found the police station. It was a one-story stucco building with a flat roof. There was a concrete staircase leading to a concrete front entry porch. A handicap walkway switches back and forth and terminates at the side of the porch.

One enters the building through the large glass entry door. There is a waiting area running the full width of the building in the front. At the back of the waiting area, there is a long desk manned by the desk sergeant. There were chairs and benches along the inside of the front exterior wall.

They went to the desk sergeant. Rick said, "Hi, I would like to report a possible kidnapping."

The sergeant replied, "How is a kidnapping a possible kidnapping. It is either a kidnapping, and if you do not have evidence of a kidnapping, it is a missing person's case."

Rick, not wanting to quibble, replied, "Okay. I would like to report a missing person's case."

The desk sergeant picked up his phone and spoke with someone who, Rick presumed, was on site.

We were asked to sit down and wait to be called.

After a few minutes, an officer came out of the back area and into the area behind the long desk. He looked over at us and asked if we were the ones reporting the missing person. Rick said that we were. As we rose, the officer asked that only one of us come back to make the report. Rick went.

Rick and the officer passed through a door and entered the area located on the other side of the wall from the reception area. In this area, there were several steel desks facing one another. There was a chair behind each desk, and another chair along the side each desk. The officer led Rick over to his desk and asked that he sit down in the chair next to it.

The officer asked, "So, you have a missing person situation. Please tell me about it."

I started, "I was on a business trip in Newport Beach. I called my wife at 6 in the morning, and she did not answer. I called my neighbor. She told me that my wife's car was not in the driveway. I went to my wife's office to see if her car was there. It was. My wife was not in the building, and the building was officially closed because it was Saturday.

"When my wife's car was found at her office, I determined that she was taken by someone and is now missing. I know that proper protocol is to contact the local authorities, which is what I am doing. It is my understanding that they are required to report to the Department of Justice."

The officer said, "Let me get this straight. She has been missing since this morning. You do realize that she's been missing for less than a few hours. By law, we don't take reports until a person has been missing for 24 to 48 hours."

Rick snapped, "I'm an attorney, and not a complete idiot. You know perfectly well that there is no longer a waiting period before reporting a missing person. Missing persons are now to be reported immediately. This delay tactic might work with some people, but I am not one of those people. I demand to make a report now, and I mean right now."

Rick was not happy.

The officer gave Rick a missing persons' form which he filled out. He left the form with the officer and left, knowing that not much would come of it. He was starting to get the feeling that there were business interests which influenced the local police. Hard to rock the boat with a company that employees more than half the people in a small town.

Before leaving Rick asked, "Are there any traffic cameras out on the interstate on the way to Three Palms?"

The officer replied, "I doubt it. Nobody goes out there. Why?"

Rick said, "I need to see if there were any large trucks out there last night between around 8 p.m. on Friday and 2 a.m. on Saturday, particularly a caravan of three trucks."

The officer said that he would check and let me know. Rick gave him his cell phone number. Their business was done. Rick said goodbye and left.

Rick, Moose, Lester, and Dave left the police station and returned to Rick's car. On the way back Moose asked, "Anything of interest happen in there?"

Rick, who was now becoming as economical with his words as Moose, replied, simply, "No." Nothing else was said on the trip to Amanda's.

Rick, Moose, Lester, and Dave drove the 25 minutes or so necessary to reach Amanda's house. It was on the outskirts of Fairview in a nice, clean neighborhood not far from the downtown area and the AG's office at which she worked.

They reached the front door. They could hear Amanda inside. She seemed to be crying hysterically. Rick knocked on the door. Amanda opened it and let the four of them in. The four men and Amanda were standing in the entry. She had been crying but was trying to pull herself back together.

Rick asked her what happened. She replied, "Just after Bart got here, I thought I heard something outside. I looked out the window and saw two security-guard types dressed in blue blazers and grey slacks outside with guns drawn. I panicked. Bart told me to calm down. He said that he would take care of it. He went outside. I heard a commotion, and the next thing I saw was Bart dragging these two huge guys through the living room and into the front bedroom. He tied them up and told me to relax. He said that it was under control."

Moose said, "Poor guys."

Rick asked, "Where is Bart now?"

Amanda replied, "He's in the living room."

Rick walked from the entry to the living room. He could see Bart sitting on the couch reading the newspaper. There was a cup of coffee on the coffee table in front of him. He looked normal and relaxed.

Rick asked Bart, "What's going on?"

Bart replied, "Nothing. I saw two guys outside of the house with guns so I went out and brought them in. I put them in the front bedroom."

Rick, Moose, Lester, and Dave looked into the front bedroom. They saw the two guys who had been stripped of not only their weapons but also of their clothes. They were tied up in their underwear and were huddled in a corner of the room.

The two guys, even two large armed guys, were barely a match for Bart. He was an ex-Ranger who now taught hand to hand combat, as the Army decided that his killing ability had become too rigorous.

According to Amanda, she looked out of the window and saw Bart disarmed them with a couple of quick moves and then beat the living daylights out of both of them. (Bart would never speak of an apprehension. It was something that just happened, and it was generally not pretty.) She said that he tied them up and brought them inside. He put them in the front bedroom.

When the front bedroom door was opened, the two men could be seen tied up. They actually looked happy to see us, for which I do not blame them. I had seen Bart in action when we were rescuing Taylor and Tammy from the gangster's compound, and it was pretty scary, even when I knew that he was on my side.

Though we would now have to figure out what we were going to do with the two guys, on balance, they were a great benefit. For one thing, we could find out for whom they were working and where a kidnapped person might be held. Also, we had their clothes if we wanted to infiltrate the place where Taylor was being held.

Moose, Lester, and I went into the bedroom and closed the door. Moose thought that bringing Bart in so soon might be too much for them.

Moose calmly said the following: "We have been to Three Palms and are certain that there was an illegal dumping operation there. As Amanda works for the Attorney General in environmental law, it would be too much of a coincidence for you fellows to show up here unless you thought that she might have information about the dumping. This means that it is likely that you are working for the person who perpetrated the illegal dumping.

"I have two very simple questions for you. If you answer these questions truthfully, no harm will come to you. Otherwise, I will have no alternative but to re-introduce you to my friend Bart, and sometimes his manners are not terrific, as I think you already know.

"The first question is who hired you to come here to question Amanda? The second question is where can we find this person right now? Pretty simple."

The first guard answered. "We are not going to tell you anything. We demand to be taken to the police."

Moose replied, "While I agree that the police would be a pleasant respite for you, you will not be taken there until we get the information we need from you. And you can trust that the process by which this will be done will be painful, long, and arduous. It has been rumored that some people have actually had an allergic reaction to our form of questioning and have, unfortunately, died. I hope that this does not happen to you. I like you guys, and it seems like you were just doing your job."

The second security guard said, "Please don't hurt us. We don't know anything to tell you."

Moose said, "Let us be the judge of that. You see the wife of Rick over here has been kidnapped, and we need to know where to find her. We will be finding out one way or another. We're just hoping that it will be sooner rather than later as time is of the essence."

The first security guard said, "We had nothing to do with any kidnapping. Please let us go."

Moose said, "So then what were your instructions when you came here to see Amanda. Were you asked to come by to find out if she needed anything from the market? My guess is that you were tasked with finding out what she knew about the illegal dumping. So, excuse me if we are not planning to go easy on you when you lie to us."

Moose, Lester, and Rick left the bedroom and returned to the living room. Moose said that he would extract the information out of one or the other of the them but that it might take some time, and it was already getting late.

He figured that whatever they had planned for Taylor would probably take place in the evening when it was dark, as darkness hides a multitude of sins when it comes to murder. As a result, they did not have much time to find out if, where, and by whom she was being held and to devise a plan to extricate her. Unfortunately, as we all know too well, Moose is almost always right about matters of the sword.

Rick said to Moose, "Do you mind if I have a crack at these two? I have a couple of ideas which might speed up the process."

Moose looked at Lester and Bart, who seemed okay with it, and said, "Okay, give it a shot."

Without saying so, one would believe that Moose thought that Rick's personal interest might work to their advantage. Rick, below a thinly veiled façade, was mad as hell, and Moose sensed it.

Rick first went into the garage and grabbed a hammer, a screw driver, and an 18-inch-long chain he found.

When he entered the front bedroom and was out of ear-shot, Dave asked Moose, "Why do you think he needs that stuff. Is he going to fix a shelf?"

Bart replied for Moose, "No Dave. No shelves will be fixed. I think he has other ideas."

And he did.

Rick entered the room. He said to the first guard, "The woman you came here to kidnap or kill is a very good friend of my wife's. My wife does not make friends easily, and if she thought that this person was worthy of her friendship, then she must be a very special person indeed. Let me tell you that my wife would be so very disappointed in both of you if she thought you meant to harm her friend.

"That said, if my wife were here, I would not feel bad about turning her loose on you. If you thought that Bart was bad, trust me, my wife would be much worse. Compared to my wife, being with Bart would be like sitting on Santa's lap.

"My wife would start by breaking both of your legs and arms. If that didn't do it, she would tear the eyeballs out of their sockets, which I hear is quite painful and can lead to blindness and even death.

"But you guys are lucky. You just have me, and I am truly a pussycat compared to her. So, tell me, for whom are you working, and where we can find him."

The first guard replied, "We're not telling you anything."

Just then, Rick drew back the hammer and hit the table next to the hand of the second guard. He was visibly shaken.

Rick said, "Here is my plan. I've heard that it is quite effective and almost always gets results. Here goes: I am going to beat one of you to death. You will be afforded the opportunity to decide which one of the two of you will die first. When one of you watches the other die, you will be much more likely to give me the information I need. It's an old Indian trick. You see, when one hostage sees the other die, he recognizes how serious his interrogator really is."

Both of the guys were tied to wooden chairs. As time was important, Moose came in to see how things were going. Rick hit the second guard so hard that he and his chair went flying across the room.

The second guard said to Moose, "Can't you say something to stop him?"

Moose replied, "I'm afraid that if I say anything, he might get mad." Moose left the room.

Rick then took the chain, folded it into his palm creating a 10-inch loop. He banged the table next to the first guard so hard that he could feel the wind from the chain on his hand.

Moose, Lester, Bart, and Dave were sitting in the living room just outside of the bedroom door. Dave asked, "What do you think he is doing in there?"

Moose said, "I'm certain that he is using some of the more persuasive arguments that he learned in law school."

While waiting in the living room, Lester and Bart were going through the wallets of the two guys. There was not much. Just directions to Amanda's house.

A few minutes later Rick came out of the bedroom. Moose asked, "Anything?"

Rick, now also becoming a man of few words, said only, "Allied Chemical."

Moose replied, "Makes sense. A chemical company. Dave checked all three chemical companies on google. Allied has a main corporate office in Lakeside, but it has a plant out in the desert fairly close to Three Palms. Seems like an obvious place for illegal dumping. The other two companies were closer to other possible dumping areas.

But where would they keep Taylor, the corporate office or the plant?"

Dave was still a little perplexed about Rick's questioning. He asked, "How did you get them to tell you where she was?"

Rick replied, "I guess they had a crisis of conscience."

With the question of where she would be kept still unanswered, Moose asked the first guard at which facility Taylor might be held.

The first guard answered, "I am not going to say."

Moose replied, "Fine with me. Rick was just getting warmed up."

The second guard, really scared, interjected, "No, not him again. At the corporate office in Lakeside."

Moose interjected, "See how easy that was."

They two guards were still in their underwear. Rick gave them some clothes he packed for his trip which he had in his car. He kept their clothes for future possible use.

They loaded the two guards into the van that Bart was driving when he was dispatched to Amanda's. Moose did a switch. He had Lester drive the van with the two guards and had Bart come with him, Rick, and Dave in Rick's suburban. Direct orders concerning strategy made by Moose were not questioned, ever. They were only followed.

Rick said to Amanda, "Do you have a dark blue business suit about the color of the blazers they were wearing?"

"Yes."

"Please put it on. You will be coming with us."

Amanda asked, "Why?"

Rick said, "For two reasons. For one, you will be safer with us than you will be here, and, secondly, we will need you to play an Allied receptionist. You'll see."

Moose and Bart were about the same size as the two guys. They put on their clothes. Rick had a blue blazer in his car. Dave was already wearing a blue blazer with grey slacks. Lester would be the outside man. He would remain dressed as he was. Amanda came out from her master bedroom in a dark blue business suit. She looked perfect.

Rick, Moose, Bart, Dave, and Amanda went in Rick's Suburban. Lester took the two guards in his van. They drove towards Lakeside.

They knew where they were going - the Allied Chemical building in Lakeside. They were not certain whether Taylor was being held there, though they figured that she probably was. If she was there, they were not certain exactly how they were going to extricate her. They would have to develop a plan when they saw the building and consider the problems that it presented.

They were on route to Lakeside where Taylor spent the night in a cage.

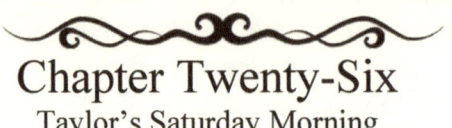

Chapter Twenty-Six
Taylor's Saturday Morning

Taylor woke up from a restless sleep at 7 a.m. Unknown to her, she was sleeping on a cot in a cage located on the 4th parking level of the underground parking garage under the corporate office tower of Allied Chemical.

She was groggy from being hit on the head and knocked out and then being given a sedative to calm her down.

When she awoke, she was startled. She immediately tried to sit up, but she was handcuffed to the cot's frame.

One of the several security guards for the building was in the cage with her. He was assigned to watch her and to report when she awoke. Her reputation preceded her. Even when locked in the cage, they were afraid of what she might do.

She spoke to the guard and asked, "Where am I?"

The guard replied, "You are in a cage in an underground parking garage."

"Why am I here?"

The guard answered, "You are here because it is suspected that you witnessed illegal activity."

She asked, "Isn't finding illegal activity a good thing?"

The guard said, "Maybe usually, but not in this case."

She asked, "What do you mean?"

The guard answered, "That is all above my pay grade. Someone else will come and tell you all about it in a couple of hours."

The guard continued, "I have been asked to have you change out of your clothes and into this jumpsuit I have here. There are also canvas shoes for you."

The guard was holding a folded orange jumpsuit and the shoes. We took the liberty of measuring you last night while you were sleeping. The thought sent a chill down her spine.

"Why the jumpsuit?"

"I really don't know. I was only asked to have you put it on and to take the clothes you are wearing."

He placed long, plastic gloves over each hand and forearm and handed her the jumpsuit and shoes. He indicated that she could change behind a curtain hanging in the corner just outside of the cage. She changed into the jump suit. She took off her shoes and replaced them with the canvas shoes. She handed him her clothes and shoes. He carefully placed her clothes and shoes into a large, thick plastic bag.

"By the way, my name is Jose. I am one of the security guards working here in the building. Would you like something to eat?"

"Yes. That would be good."

She figured that she would be as cooperative with this guard as possible. He appeared to not know anything anyway. Also, if she seemed docile, he might let his defenses down which might provide an opportunity to escape. If she started out belligerent, he might exert more control or ask for another guard, neither of which would be to her advantage.

It was coming up on late morning. She knew that she would eventually learn who was in charge which would give her only a couple of hours until they would have to get rid of her, one way of the other.

The guard brought her breakfast consisting of scrambled eggs, ham, toast, and orange juice. She asked for and received tea instead of coffee. She was too hungry to pass on breakfast. Also, she thought that the relaxed nature of the cleanup of the breakfast dishes might provide an opportune time to work her way towards the cage door and that one of the utensils necessary to eat might provide a small weapon of sorts.

Without the food service, the downtime while she was sitting and he was watching would not provide any distractions necessary for an escape. To negotiate an escape, they would have to be doing something such as eating, cleaning up, or her going to the bathroom.

She felt badly because she actually rather liked this guard, but to escape it would probably become necessary to give him a real beat-down. If he survived, and she escaped, his boss might kill him for incompetence. But she knew what she had to do.

She was finished with breakfast. It was time for the guard to collect the dishes and utensils. It was her opportunity to escape.

The guard collected her dirty dishes and most of the utensils. She managed to hide a short, dull knife. As she suspected, he was so concerned with balancing the dishes that he stopped paying attention to his primary duty – watching her.

As we know, she went on a camping trip with Moose, Bart, and the boys several years ago where she learned, among other things, about guns, hand to hand combat, and waterboarding. She had a couple of refresher courses over the year and often went to a boxing gym to keep her skills in shape. For her size, she could pack a punch. She knew that if she was to escape now, she would need to use all of her skills.

When the guard opened the cage door to take the dishes out, she made her move.

She over-powered the guard quickly. She moved in behind and put a strangle-hold around his neck to the point where he passed out. She did not kill him, though this would have been possible and would probably have been to her advantage. Was she getting a little soft?

Chapter Twenty-Seven
Taylor's Saturday Mid-Day to Afternoon

Though she was out of the cage, her battle was still less than half done. She still had to get out of the parking garage. She did not know how many levels there were in the garage or how the levels were staffed. Fortunately for her it was Saturday, and there would not be many cars in the garage, and the regular staff would not be working. The only staff would be the security guards tasked to look after her, a receptionist or two, and two or three guards in the security room.

The two elevator doors were visible in the parking garage. These two elevators went only as far as the ground floor level. Under normal circumstances, one might breach a door and work his way up inside of the elevator shaft. However, this method was not possible as each door had an outer steel door which rolled down and was locked to the concrete floor. It appeared as if the plan was for detainees to be unable to access the elevators shafts.

She saw the ramp leading up from this parking level. She followed the ramp up to where she could see the next higher level, but the opening was blocked with another rolling steel door which was locked to the floor.

While she was inspecting the ramp, the security person guarding her regained consciousness and called his boss to tell him of the escape.

His boss, the chief of security, was a fellow by the name of Ross Johnson. When he received the call, he was in a meeting with the CEO, Mr. Sinclair, in Mr. Sinclair's private penthouse office.

Mr. Johnson was not happy. Not only would he have to go down and take care of Ms. Shaw himself, but he would have the unpleasant duty of telling Mr. Sinclair what transpired.

He hung up and said to Mr. Sinclair, "Very sorry sir, but it appears as if Ms. Shaw has escaped from the cage and is now running around the parking garage trying to figure out a way to get to the outside. This, of course, is impossible but a nuisance none the less."

Mr. Sinclair became enraged, "That cannot be. You need to get down there with Hank and Phil and get her back in her cage. I'm going to need her alive and not too badly damaged for my plan for her tonight. We must get her under control soon. I would have all four of you clowns killed if I didn't need you so much. Take the service elevator and get going."

Johnson, Hank, and Phil made their way towards the service elevator to find Jose and retrieve the girl.

On each floor, the service elevator emptied into an unfinished part of the floor. Access into the elevator could only be achieved by retinal scan and only the retinas of Sinclair (as CEO) and Johnson (as head of security), could provide that scan. All staircases in the building were shut and locked tight, notwithstanding fire codes which were disregarded.

Johnson, Hank, and Phil met at the private elevator door. Johnson applied his retina, and the door opened. Johnson directed the cab down to the 4th parking level.

At the 4th parking level, the three got out and entered the parking garage. They could see that the door to the cage was open. They found Jose. He was still a little dazed by the beating and strangulation he received. They put him back together and asked where Taylor was located. He said that she had to be somewhere on the floor, as the elevators have metal doors which lock, and the entry into the parking garage from the driveway also has a metal door which was also locked.

They decided to split up. Hank would go to the south, and Phil would go to the west. Johnson would stay with Jose for a little while, hoping that one of his men would bring her back to the cage.

Taylor was at a loss. The entire floor was underground. The only ways to reach the lobby were the two passenger elevators, the service elevator, the driveway, and the stairs. The driveway and the stairs were locked down tight. The passenger elevators were locked with metal doors brought down over the elevator doors. The service elevator required a retinal scan.

Taylor initially went south to the far south wall. She could see no means of escape from this location.

She saw Hank, the guard who went south. She snuck up behind him and grabbed him around his neck. He fought her off and squared off in front of her. He went for his walkie, and she kicked it out of hand.

He took a wild swing with his right hand. She blocked it with her left arm. Now his face was open. She took a full right-hand swing at his face, knocking him to the concrete floor. She stomped his face, stomach, and below his waist.

He somehow got up. She grabbed his neck from behind and choked him until he became unconscious. She tied him up with his belt.

As she moved to the west, she encountered Phil. She snuck up and grabbed him around the neck from behind. She knocked the walkie off of his belt. He put up a pretty good struggle, but she subdued him. She tied him up as well as she could.

Her only play at this point was to return to the cage entrance to see if one of the guards stayed behind with Jose. It turned out that one did, and it was Johnson. Johnson looked more formidable than Hank, Phil, and Jose. She thought that he might be the chief of security, which was the case.

While in the back of the garage, she saw the entry door to the security elevator. Just to the left of the door, she could see a retinal scan screen.

Chapter Twenty-Eight
Taylor's Saturday Late Afternoon

She could see that Johnson was answering a call on his walkie-talkie. He seemed to be talking to his boss, as his tone was generally conciliatory.

He spoke into the walkie and said, "Very sorry boss. We know she's in here, but we cannot find her. Hank and Phil have been out looking, but I haven't heard a word from either of them. I hope they're okay. Judging from what she did to Jose here she must have some kind of martial arts training we didn't know about."

Sinclair responded, "It's late afternoon now. I need to have her dressed and ready by dark, which is around 7 or so. If you can't get her up here by then, I will have to call out more men, but that will take time. I have Trey here. I can send him down too."

Johnson said, "Don't worry boss. We will have her to you by then. I'll let you know about Trey. I don't think we'll need him right now anyway."

Johnson, not unlike many employee types, knew better than to ask why Sinclair needed her by dark. He would just try to do what he was told. It looked as if it would take all four of them together to round her up.

Johnson and Jose took off looking for Hank and Phil. They found both of them and untied them. They then moved in a pack to try to find Taylor. The floor area of the garage, while large, was not overwhelming, and there were no cars behind which to hide.

Johnson finally saw Taylor out of the corner of his eye. The four of them formed a circle around her. She fought them off. Hank grabbed her from behind. Phil moved in as if he was going to punch her. She was able to kick him in the face which sent him flying backwards.

Johnson got ahold of her. She wrestled away from him and gave him an open hand punch to the jaw. She grabbed his mouth and eyes. He cried out in pain.

He got away and hit her over the head with a night stick he brought. This put her out cold.

The four of them carried her to the service elevator. Johnson used his retina to gain entry. The four of them took her up to the penthouse to see Mr. Sinclair.

From the service elevator, they entered the finished part of the penthouse through a back door. Johnson asked Sinclair where he should take her. Sinclair said to take her to his office.

Chapter Twenty-Nine
Taylor's Saturday Very Late Afternoon

The four men looked pretty beaten up. She too was badly beaten with bruises on her face and body. Even so, she looked very beautiful and even serene. Sinclair thought to himself what a waste to have such a beautiful woman working as an attorney in crime prevention. She should be home being taken care of by a rich guy. Obviously, he did not know her at all.

With her beauty and intelligence, she could be with any guy she wanted and never have to work. But she did not operate that way. She wanted a life with purpose. She wanted to contribute. She chose a guy who supported her efforts rather than one who would constantly try to tear her down so that he could feel better about himself. She wanted a partner, and with Rick, she clearly had that. He worshiped the ground she walked on, and she wouldn't have it any other way.

Sinclair's thinking was from a different era, an era in which rich white men controlled everything, including women. Sorry Mr. Sinclair, that ship has sailed. Guess you will have to learn the hard way.

She had now been placed in a chair in Sinclair's office opposite his huge desk.

He asked, "Would you like a little time to freshen up?"

She replied, "No."

Sinclair said, "Okay then let me cut to the chase. Trey here tells me that you two witnessed some dumping at Three Palms where it appeared as if one of the drivers died. Is that true?"

"Yes. That is true."

"How do you know he was dead."

She replied, "With a question like that, you must be dumber than you look. It would be most unusual to put a life-less body into a barrel and put the barrel back into the truck from which it came, if the person put in the barrel was not dead. Even if the person put in the barrel was not dead then, he would certainly be dead by now."

Sinclair asked, "What would you have had them do?"

"That should be obvious even to an idiot such as you. You call 911 and ask for an ambulance. It's not rocket science."

Sinclair responded, "I'm the CEO of a major public company. I don't do things that way."

Taylor was becoming a little unhinged, which, unfortunately, is often her way. She said, "Yes you are the CEO of a major public company. As such, you have this lavish office. I'm sure you drive a fancy car. You probably have a few houses, one out here in the middle of the nowhere and one in a normal place like Los Angeles or New York. I'm sure you have a wife, as there are many women who are so desperate for security that they will even sleep with a creep like you. Must be a very rewarding life for them."

"Shut your mouth, or I'm going to come over there and slap you."

Taylor replied, "You have no idea how much I would love it if you did that. I would so delight in beating the daylights out of you. Without these clowns you call security guards and your so-called investigator who can't investigate his way out of a paper bag, you are nothing."

"I'm the boss here."

Taylor replied, "No. You are the CEO, I will grant you that, but you might not own a single share of stock in Allied Chemical. You're just a cover boy for the shareholders. Shareholders expect a soft white guy from a rich family to be CEO. You probably can't do one thing that this business does. The lowest level lab technician has more skills than you.

"You just have a degree from the right school. You probably make 200 times a year more than the rank and file employees, and they do the actual work. You can't mix the simplest chemical compound that this company sells. The only thing you can mix is a bad martini."

Sinclair countered, "Remember, you are speaking to the CEO of Allied Chemical."

Taylor responded, "You may be that today, but when you get convicted of loading the life-less body of one of your truck drivers into a barrel of poison, you will no longer be CEO of anything, except maybe Cell Block C.

"And even if no criminal indictment is handed down, you are through. No public company will have a monster such as you as its public face. You won't be able to get a job in the mail room even if every allegation against you cannot be proven and is just innuendo."

Sinclair responded, "I'm not going to let that happen. I'll sweep this under the rug."

Taylor said, "You must have one hell of a PR firm then. Besides, I will be around to testify loudly and clearly against you."

Sinclair answered, "I truly doubt that."

Taylor responded, "Even if you get rid of me, my husband and our friends will hunt you down to the end of your days. You will never have a single night's sleep again, ever."

Sinclair replied, "Originally, I brought you up here to find out whether you told anyone what you think you saw out at Three Palms. I don't think you told anyone anything. Trey said that after you witnessed the events, he hit you over the head and knocked you out before you could even use your phone. He finally did one thing right. As we both know, Trey is an incompetent fool. I will have to get rid of him anyway so I don't have to worry about him trying to do anything stupid in the future, like blackmail."

Taylor said, "I agree with the part about Trey being a fool. He certainly is. He only knocked me out because I didn't see it coming. But I believe that you have sadly misjudged my husband and our friends. Trust me when I tell you that they will make this right. These guys are so scary that they will crush you and your inept rent-a-cops without hesitation."

Sinclair replied, "He doesn't even know where you are or what has happened to you, and he has no way of finding out. According to my research, he's nothing but a small-time deputy DA in a small time DA's office in the middle of nowhere. A minor public sector employee going up against the CEO of a major public corporation. He has no chance. He's probably chasing his tail someplace in the desert. And just in case you said anything to your girlfriend Amanda, I have taken care of her already."

Taylor replied, "If you so much as touch a hair on her head, it will lay down a beating on you that you will never forget. Trust me."

Johnson entered the room. He asked, "What do you want me to do with her boss?"

Sinclair answered, "Take her into the study, tie her up, and don't let her move. If she gets away from you, you're done."

Taylor was taken into the study and tied up. All four security guards took up posts. Trey came into Sinclair's office.

Trey asked, "What are you going to do with her?"

Sinclair said, "You'll see."

It was early evening, and the sun was about to set. Sinclair had been waiting all day for night to fall. He knew that night would mean that most of the people would have cleared out of the building, except for two people at the reception desk and three in the security room monitoring the video feeds. Darkness would provide perfect cover for his outdoor activities – his party on the roof.

Chapter Thirty
Saturday Night - Allied Chemical Corporate Office Building

Sinclair was a desperate man. Losing his CEO position would ruin him in so many ways. He would lose his job, his several houses, his several cars, and probably his wife, unless she turned out to be someone completely different than even he thought she was. Further, he probably would wind up in prison. Rough stakes for a soft white guy.

His only way out was to silence Taylor for good, which means that he had no alternative but to kill her.

Fortunately, Rick was driving his big Suburban. He had enough room for himself and the four other people with him. He still had his gear from his tactical training. Lester was taking the two security guards they apprehended in the van.

They reached the building. It was impressive. Such a tall modern looking building in the middle of nowhere. They pulled into the guest parking. Rick and Dave were already dressed similarly to the Allied employees. Moose and Bart were wearing the clothes they had taken from the two guards who came to Amanda's house which were similar to the clothes Rick and Dave had on. Lester was in his own clothes, but he would remain outside.

Rick went to the front door, which was locked. The door and the front wall were glass. He could see two receptionists, one male and one female, at two computer terminals. He knocked on the door and waived at the receptionists. The female buzzed him in thinking that he was going to take over her shift so she could go home for the day.

Though their replacement would usually have a key, she must have thought that he forgot his. They often use temps, and besides Rick looked like someone who would be working for a large company. Rick crossed the lobby and went over to the reception desk.

Rick was a good-looking guy, and the receptionist may have given him a little more leeway than she would have given someone who was not as good looking, including letting him in without a key or a badge.

She said to him, "Hi. Did you forget your key?"

Rick replied, "No. And I am so very sorry to tell you this. My friends and I are taking over this entire building right now, including the reception desk and the security room."

Bart had already picked the lock to the side door. He and Moose gained access to the security room, overpowered the three guards, tied them up, and placed them in the security room closet.

Rick brought the female and male receptionists into the security room and placed them in the security room closet. He went out and found Dave in the lobby and brought him into the security room.

Amanda, who was dressed similarly to the female receptionist, was brought to the reception desk. She would stay there and pretend to be an Allied receptionist.

In the security room, Dave went to work on the computer finding the floor plans for the various floors and the access points, which were limited.

Rick, Moose, and Bart remained in the security room while Dave was working on the computer, and Amanda was working the reception desk.

Lester brought the two security guards from Amanda's house from the van into the building through the front door. He found a janitor's closet. He tied them up and put them in the janitor's closet.

It was dusk, and Rick knew that time was of the essence. Rick was ready to address the assembled group of detainees as follows:

"It appears as if last night my wife witnessed employees of Allied Chemical make an illegal toxic waste dump in a place called Three Palms. Three Palms is located in the middle of the desert about 20 or 30 minutes away from the Allied chemical plant. Unfortunately, in addition to the illegal dumping, one of the drivers died from exposure to hydrogen sulfide. My wife witnessed his death as well, it appears.

"Because of her knowledge, she was apprehended and brought to this building. I do not know where she is being kept. My computer specialist is going through the tapes, and we expect to know her whereabouts fairly soon, unless one of you knows and is willing to tell us.

"We mean you no harm. If we wanted you dead, trust me, you would already be dead. These gentlemen with me are decorated Army Rangers and have seen much action during war time the exact nature of which none of us wishes to know. They too are my wife's friends.

"It is my opinion that the CEO of this company, because he stands to have his life reduced from one of exceptional luxury to one confined to a jail cell, will become desperate enough to kill my wife.

"Please allow me to tell you now that this will happen only over my dead body and the dead bodies of anyone who stands in my way. And I mean that will all sincerity. My wife is the love of my life, and she and I will do anything to protect our relationship.

"If any of you has any information about my wife and her whereabouts or about any abnormalities or odd features of this building, please tell me now, as any information will save time, and time is something I do not have."

When Rick concluded, the staff people in the closet were noticeably shaken.

Dave chimed in, "I think I may have something Rick."

Rick asked, "What do you have?"

Dave went on, "The video shows that the parking garage is four levels deep but that only the upper three levels are used for parking. The driveway down to the fourth level has a separate metal gate which is now closed and locked."

The female receptionist, who was the person who was the most helpful, said, "No one is allowed to go to the 4th level. I don't think that there are even cameras down there."

Rick said, "It might be worth a look. Do the elevators go that far?"

The receptionist replied, "I don't think so, but it is possible." (Actually, the two elevators from the parking levels to the lobby do go to the 4th level.)

Dave replied, "One camera caught a glimpse, must have been by accident, of someone who looks similar to the way you described your wife to me."

Rick asked, "Why do you think it was by accident."

Dave said, "It appeared to have been taken in an unfinished part of the building outside of an elevator door. For a brief second, the camera caught a glimpse of a woman being dragged either into or out of an elevator. The feed to the camera then was quickly turned off."

"When was that?"

Dave answered, "Not too long ago. Maybe 20 minutes."

Rick asked, "Does anyone know about an unfinished part of the building."

One of the security guards answered, "There is a service elevator in the building. It is separate from the passenger elevators and is located in the far rear of the building. On each floor, there is a separate area for each service elevator door. Each of these areas is located in an unfinished part of the building and is separated from the finished part of the building by a false wall. This allows one to use the service elevator without being seen from the finished part of the floor where people are working. It is rumored that the service elevator requires a retinal scan to operate.

"The service elevator runs to the 15th floor, which is the penthouse level. Similar to the other floors, the service elevator opens into an unfinished part of the building behind a false wall. On the other side of the false wall, there is the finished penthouse."

Rick went on, "They must have been keeping her in the 4th level parking and then they brought her to the penthouse to find out whether she knows anything. Whether she does or does not with everything that has transpired, they will have no alternative but to dispose of her. Not good."

Moose weighed in, "They must be taking her to the roof. He's not going to mess up his penthouse office with a killing and a dead body. My guess is that he will take her to the roof."

Rick thought to himself, "Unfortunately, Moose is almost always right about these things."

Another security guard added, "That makes sense. You see there is no access to the roof except by a private elevator in the penthouse. You cannot get to the roof by any other elevator, even the service elevator. This makes the roof a perfect place to commit a crime."

The female receptionist spoke, "I don't know if this is of any help, but a guy I did not recognize as working here came through the lobby. He was not dressed like an Allied employee. He was wearing an open black shirt, grey slacks, and black leather shoes. He had a gold chain around his neck and a couple of gold rings. Way too flashy for Allied.

"He thought he was a player. He was checking out everything in a skirt. He lamely tried to hit on me. He said that he was an investigator for the Attorney General and was in town on an important assignment. He said that he had an evening rooftop meeting with the CEO which he thought would be short. He said that after his meeting, he would like to take me out for a drink. The hardest part of declining was trying to determine which of my dozen or so excuses I would use.

"I told him that I had to see my mother in the hospital after work and that he could come along if he wished.

"He passed. Works every time. He's really not interesting."

Rick said, "That is great help. I'm pretty sure I know who that is. I think it's Trey, my wife's investigator. I think we can narrow it down to the roof in the evening. He probably wants Trey there so he can dispose of him at the same time. He would be way too much of a loose end. Thank you. That was great help."

Rick addressed his guys, "Well, I see what I need to do."

Moose, a little surprised by Rick's statement said inquisitively, "And what might that be. There is no roof access except by private elevator which can be accessed by retina scan only."

Rick said, "Here is my plan. I am going to find an office on the 14th floor with a window on the west side of the building. I am going to cut an opening in this window, climb up the outside of the building, throw down two ropes for you and Bart, and do what I need to do to get Taylor."

Moose could only say, "You must be out of your freaking mind. That's impossible."

Rick and Dave looked over the floor plan for the 14th floor. They found an office with a window on the west side. The private elevator from the penthouse comes up on the east side so it stands to reason that most of the action involving Taylor and the bad guys would be taking place on the east side of the roof near the elevator. Rick said that this means that they will have to get onto the roof on the west side. There is some AC equipment which would provide cover.

Dave said to the group, "You know that there is a heliport on the roof in the rear east corner behind the popup for the private elevator shaft and door. What is the plan if this guy dispatches a para-military group from a helicopter or tries to use a helicopter for his escape?"

Moose said that he needed to ask Lester, his arms guy, whether there was a way to take down a helicopter with a weapon that they could get up onto the roof. Moose called Lester, who was still outside.

Moose put Lester on speaker and asked, "How could we persuade a helicopter to not land. Would we need a big gun?"

Lester replied, "No. A helicopter is a delicately balanced machine with much of its mass concentrated around the engine. When the main rotor above the cabin spins, the entire craft wants to spin. The second rotor located at the tail end is designed to keep the entire helicopter from spinning so that the main rotor will provide lift.

"If you want to disable a helicopter, all you need to do is shoot at the tail, which is generally made of fiberglass or hollow aluminum. If the bullet strikes just the right place, it disables the rear rotor. When this happens, the rear rotor will be unable to stop the helicopter from spinning. This will make it impossible to operate the craft, and the pilot will have no alternative but to bug out. This can be done with a handgun.

"So, the short answer to your question is that you don't need a big gun to take down a helicopter. But you do need a gun, like a hand gun, and you do need a bullet that is fired in exactly the right place. The trick here is that to fire the bullet in just the right place, you will need someone who is not just a good shot, but you will need someone who is an expert marksman."

Moose replied, "Got it."

Moose's marksmanship was legend, and questions about who would be taking the shot were not even entertained.

Rick, Moose, and Bart went to the pre-determined 14th floor office. They found the west side window that they would be using. Lester was to exit from the building and go around to the east side, staying close enough to the building to keep from being seen from the roof.

Once in the 14th floor office, Rick laid out the things he brought. He brought two heavy duty glass hand suction devices, a professional glass cutter, what appeared to Moose to be a climbing vest, his Glock, a bungee cord, and two thick ropes.

Rick found a window he liked. He scribed a 4-foot by 4-foot square on the inner glass. The glass for a high rise building typically consists of two panes separated by an air space. Each pane is a quarter inch thick. The air space between the panes is ½ inch wide. This makes the entire assembly approximately 1 inch thick.

Rick cut the first pane and used the suction cups to bring the piece into the office. He repeated the process with the outer piece. This left a 4 by 4-foot hole in the window to the outside.

Rick put on his vest and placed the bungee cord and both ropes over his shoulder and under his opposite arm. The bungee and ropes were equipped with firm hooks on one end.

Rick exited the hole in the window and began a vertical climb up the outside glass skin using the suction cups. The suction cups had hand pumps allowing the air to be removed from the area between the rubber and the glass.

Moose and Bart looked on in amazement.

Once on the roof, Rick hooked each rope onto the railing and threw both ropes down the outside of the building.

Moose and Bart were able to grab the ropes and use them to climb up the outside of the building and onto the roof. Nice to have friends who can actually do something.

Chapter Thirty-One
Sinclair on the Roof

Before Rick, Moose, and Bart reached the roof and while Sinclair, Trey, Taylor, and Sinclair's guards were still in his penthouse office, Sinclair asked Taylor to change back into her clothes, which she did gladly. Her hands were tied and her legs were bound together with plastic coated rope.

The two men working on her, Johnson and Hank, were wearing plastic coated gloves which extended up to their armpits.

Once bound, Sinclair ordered Trey to wrestle Taylor into the elevator. Sinclair used a scan of his retina to access the elevator and to advance the cab to the roof. Once the elevator stopped at roof level, the door opened. Sinclair ordered Trey to grab Taylor around her entire body and pull her onto the roof just outside of the elevator door.

Rather than just throwing the two of them off of the roof, Sinclair decided he would tell everyone how smart he was and give them a brief address about how he planned this whole affair.

This turned out to be a good thing as it gave Rick, Moose, and Bart more time to get onto the roof. Additionally, it allowed Sinclair to incriminate himself further, which might not have even been necessary. As with everything Sinclair does, self-aggrandizement was more important than actually getting something done.

Sinclair, addressing Taylor, Trey, Johnson, Hank, Phil, and Jose, said the following:

"My job at Allied Chemical depends on keeping the stock price as high as possible. To do this, I have to make sure that Allied has maximum earnings. To maximize earnings, it sometimes become necessary to cut a few corners. It is war, and as with any war, there is going to be collateral damage.

"If we complied with all of the EPA's rules about toxic waste dumping, our earnings would be diminished which would reduce our stock price. That is unacceptable.

"We came up with a way to dispose of some of our toxic waste by dumping it way out in the desert at Three Palms.

"Though we knew that many of these loads contained dangerous hydrogen sulfide gas, we needed to redirect our resources to other parts of the business rather than using perfectly good money just to protect our workers. Unfortunately, this led to the death of an employee during a recent toxic waste dump.

"But we cannot allow this unfortunate death to derail an entire enterprise. An enterprise which supports a whole community.

"So rather than allowing Taylor to report the illegal dumping and the unfortunate death that she witnessed, we will need to dispose of her for the greater good. Sadly, we will also need to dispose of Trey, as he has learned too much.

"In a few minutes, I will have Hank throw Taylor from the roof to her certain death. I will have Johnson throw Trey from the roof. Taylor's dead body will be covered with Trey's DNA. We will maintain that Trey and Taylor were lovers, that they were having their differences, and that they asked Johnson if they could use the roof to talk. Once on the roof, a quarrel broke out, and they both accidentally fell off of the roof and died. Quite a brilliant plan, if I do say so myself."

After the remarks, Johnson had to restrain Trey, as he began to squirm after learning that he too would be thrown from the roof.

By the time Sinclair finished his speech, Rick, Moose, and Bart reached the roof and organized their equipment.

Rick directed Moose to grab Phil and Bart to grab Jose, as they had both wandered away from the others and were closer to west side of the roof.

Rick himself took off running. When Sinclair saw him, he ordered Johnson and Hank to throw Trey and Taylor off of the roof.

While running, Rick shot Sinclair in the leg. Still on the dead run, he shot Johnson, who had his gun drawn, squarely in his gun hand. Johnson still managed to throw Trey from the roof, but the gun shot to his hand prevented him from shooting back at Rick.

The commotion caused Hank to hesitate while simultaneously fighting off Taylor and trying to get his own gun drawn. Rick shot Hank in the gun hand, but Hank was still able to muscle Taylor over the railing just as Rick approached. Hank too was not able to use his gun after being shot in the hand.

Rick then did the most improbable thing that anyone may have ever done. On the dead run, he hooked the bungee cord to the railing and plunged, head first, over the side of the building.

Moose and Bart watched in amazement. Bart looked at Moose and remarked, "Well boss, it looks like we've created a monster."

Trey, who went vertically straight down was almost to the ground. Taylor, who was apparently listening to Rick when he returned from his urban training, went spread eagle, which slowed down her descent just long enough for Rick to reach her and wrap his entire body around her torso.

Just at that moment, the bungee cord reached its full length stopping them about 10 feet above the ground and then snapping back, pulling them up several feet in the air.

The bungee finally stretched itself out leaving the two of them dangling 10 feet above the ground. Lester was there waiting. He had Rick drop Taylor down to him. He laid her on the ground. He then had Rick disconnect the bungee from his vest and drop down to him.

Rick was fine. Taylor was badly shaken.

Moose and Bart were still on the roof. They rounded up Sinclair, Johnson, and Hank, all of whom were wounded, and Phil and Jose, both of whom were only badly beaten. They began to lead them to the elevator.

Just then, a helicopter commenced its descent to the heliport on the roof. This must have been the evacuation or armed support ordered by Sinclair. Moose motioned to the pilot to not land but to return to the air. The pilot did not heed his request but hovered into landing position.

Moose, using his hand gun, took a few well-placed shots at the rear rotor. This caused the craft to begin to lose control. When the rear rotor lost power, it was no longer able to keep the craft from spinning. Rather than crash land, the pilot returned to the air and flew in the direction of the closest airfield, which was not far away.

Moose and Bart moved their captives down the elevator. They found a closet on the 14th floor, the floor below the penthouse, and locked all five of them in it.

They then returned to the first-floor security room and met up with Rick, Taylor, Lester, Dave, and Amanda. Taylor and Amanda went off to another part of the room to talk. Rick could see Amanda comforting her. He was happy that she had developed a girlfriend, as she did not make friends easily. This spoke reams about Amanda.

The two guards from Amanda's house were still locked in the janitor's closet. Moose and Bart changed back into their clothes and gave the clothes they "borrowed" back to the two guards.

The two receptionists and the three guards from the security room were still in the closet in the security room.

Chapter Thirty-Two
The Police

Rick figured that to get ahead of Sinclair, it would be better if he called the police himself. This would give him the first crack at explaining what happened.

It was now very late Saturday night, and the building was empty, except for the people locked in the three closets. It is unlikely that there were any outside eye witnesses, as the building was very far from the street, and there was not much else located near the building.

Rick intended to wait for the police. Taylor and Amanda would remain with him. His idea was to first bring out the people locked in the security closet. They were generally on his side and really had no information with which to dispute his story, even if they wished to.

The much more difficult question was what to do with Moose, Bart, Dave, and Lester. He decided to let them decide if they wanted to stay or not. They chose to stay.

Eventually, he would have to bring Sinclair, Johnson, Hank, Phil, and Jose into the mix, as at least three of them would need immediate medical attention. It would be much better for him if at least one of them would confirm his story. He thought he might separate Jose out from the group and work on him, as he was the least injured and seemed to be generally the most honest.

Also, he would have to bring out the two guards who were apprehended at Amanda's house and were locked in the janitor's closet.

Interestingly enough, the most difficult part of his story would be the death of Trey. Even though his version of what happened was the exact truth, the story is so bizarre that it might not be believed without corroboration.

Rick called the police and asked for a squad car, an ambulance, and the coroner. The night was warm, and the group chose to wait outside near their parked cars. Rick killed time waiting by loading the Suburban with his gear including the ropes, the bungee cord, the bungee vest, and the glass cutter. They all had permits to carry their respective weapons.

About 10 minutes later, the police, the ambulance, and the corner showed up.

Rick addressed one of the police officers saying, "Hi. I'm Rick Miller, the person who called this in. I'm an attorney with the DA's office in Haven." (He wanted the police to know that he was an attorney and that as such, he was familiar with the law. But he also needed them to know he was a DA, and, as such, he was on their side. The police generally do not like lawyers as lawyers are more often than not on the side of the criminals.)

The officer asked, "Can you tell me what happened?"

Rick replied, "Yes. My wife here is also an attorney. She is with the State Attorney General's Office in Fairview. While still at work in her office, she received a tip that an illegal toxic waste dump was being planned by Allied Chemical in a place called Three Palms.

"As it was too late in the day to contact either the EPA or local law enforcement, she and her investigator decided to drive out to Three Palms to take a look.

"When they arrived, they saw three Allied trucks. They saw several people unloading barrels from the trucks. They saw the people remove the lids from the barrels and pour the liquid contents onto the ground.

"She saw one of the people appear to become overcome by the poisonous contents of a barrel that he had opened, fall to the ground, and apparently die. She saw some of his co-workers place his lifeless body in an empty barrel and place the barrel in one of the empty trucks.

"As it turned out, my wife's investigator was actually a mole for Allied. Before she could call the police, he hit her over the head with a night stick, and she passed out. He is the gentleman who was also thrown from the roof and is now, apparently, dead.

"When she awakened from being hit over the head, she found that she was being held prisoner in a cage on the 4th level of the underground parking garage of the Allied building, this building right here. (Rick pointed at the building next to which they were standing.)

"She was later taken to the penthouse office of the CEO. The CEO directed his security staff to take my wife and the investigator to the roof. On the roof, the CEO announced his plan to throw my wife and the investigator from the roof and say that it was the result of a lovers' quarrel which caused them to accidentally fall.

"Two members of the security staff managed to throw my wife and the investigator from the roof. I jumped from the roof attached to a bungee cord. I was able to catch my wife in mid-fall and save her, but the investigator was too far down in his descent to be saved. That is his dead body here."

The officer said, "That is truly a bizarre story. I don't see how anything like that could have actually happened."

Rick replied, "Trust me. It did."

Rick brought out the two receptionists and the three security guards from the first-floor security room. They were milling around with Moose, Bart, Lester, Dave, Amanda, and Taylor.

The officer asked, "Are these all of the people involved?"

Rick replied, "No. They are not. The CEO, the two security guards who actually threw my wife and the investigator off of the roof, and the two other security guards who were also on the roof are in a closet on the 14th floor.

"Also, there are the two guards who were dispatched by the CEO to my wife's girlfriend's home presumably to find out whether my wife contacted her about the toxic waste dumping. She and my wife work together at the Attorney General's Office. Fortunately, the two guards were apprehended and brought here. They were placed in a janitor's closet on the first floor, where they remain. They appeared willing to extract the information from my wife's girlfriend by force if necessary but were stopped from doing so by one of my friends, an ex-army ranger."

Rick went on, "To stage our rescue, we needed to replace the receptionists and the first-floor security staff with our own people. We could not leave the regular employees in place as they could inform Mr. Sinclair that there were outsiders in the building.

"We temporarily stored the two receptionists and the three first floor security guards in a closet in the security room. They were of great help to us and were in no way complicit with the CEO or with his plot against my wife. It would be great if you could dismiss them so they could go home. They've had a long day."

The officer said, "We will probably need statements from them or at least get their contact information."

The senior officer had the junior officer talk to the two receptionists and the three first floor security guards. The female receptionist offered to put together a statement to which they could all agree, if they could leave. The five of them signed the joint statement, gave their contact information, and stood by awaiting further instruction. Their statement basically said that Rick persuaded them that he needed to have his people man the reception desk and use the computers in the security room in order to save his wife and that he did no harm to them or anyone else, to their knowledge.

The coroner loaded Trey's body into his van. The ambulance arrived and was waiting for the injured.

The senior officer asked, "What about the CEO and his four security guards?"

Rick replied, "They are the people in the closet on the 14th floor."

Rick, Moose, Bart, Lester, Dave, Taylor, and Amanda accompanied the two officers to the 14th floor closet.

The senior officer opened the door. Mr. Sinclair was livid, as one might expect.

He dressed down the senior officer saying, "I am the CEO of this entire operation. I cannot believe that you left me locked in this closet, wounded for so long. I will have your badge."

The officer said that he would like to talk to him about the events of the night. Mr. Sinclair said that he would prefer to talk in his office, which was just one floor above.

Rick and his group, the two police officers, and Sinclair and his group all went up to Sinclair's penthouse office. Sinclair took up his position behind his desk.

The police officer opened the dialogue as follows: "Mr. Miller here tells me that you kidnapped his wife and threatened to kill her when she found out that you arranged for an illegal toxic waste dumping which resulted in the death of a person at Three Palms."

Sinclair retorted, "That is non-sense. I did nothing of the sort."

The officer looked at Rick and said, "Do you have any evidence to back up your story?"

Before Rick could speak, Taylor jumped in. She said, "Besides my own testimony that I was hit over the head, locked in a cage, and thrown off of the roof of a 15-story building, I have this."

She pulled out a miniature USB voice activated microphone.

She said, "When I was asked to change back into my clothes because it had Trey's DNA on it, I took this microphone out of the lead sleeve in which I keep it and put it into my non-shielded pocket. It is voice activated and good for 20 feet. It was on when Sinclair was giving his self-aggrandizing speech on the roof just before he had me thrown off. Dave, would you like to do the honors?"

Dave replied, "Certainly."

Dave found a computer in a nearby secretarial station adjacent to Mr. Sinclair's office. He took the tiny microphone and inserted it into a USB port.

Taylor said, "The recorder recorded all of Sinclair's speech while me and Trey stood on the roof waiting to be killed."

The recorder played. It was clearly Sinclair's voice. He said,

"My job at Allied Chemical depends on keeping the stock price as high as possible. To do this, I have to make sure that Allied has maximum earnings. To maximize earnings, it sometimes becomes necessary to cut a few corners. It is a war, and as with any war, there is going to be collateral damage."

The tape continued, "If we complied with all of the EPA's rules about toxic waste dumping, our earning would be diminished which would reduce our stock price. That is unacceptable."

The tape continued, "We came up with a way to dispose of some of our toxic waste by dumping it way out in the desert at Three Palms."

The tape continued, "Though we knew that many of these loads contained hydrogen sulfide, we needed to redirect our resources to other parts of the business rather than using perfectly good money just to protect our workers. Unfortunately, this led to the death of an employee during a toxic waste dump at Three Palms."

The tape continued, "But we cannot allow this unfortunate death to derail an entire enterprise. An enterprise which supports a whole community."

The tape continued, "So rather than allowing Taylor to report the illegal dumping and the unfortunate death that she witnessed, we will need to dispose of her for the greater good. Sadly, we will also need to dispose of Trey, as he has learned too much."

The tape continued, "In a few minutes, I will have Hank throw Taylor from the roof to her certain death. I will have Johnson throw Trey from the roof. Taylor's body will be covered with Trey's DNA. We will maintain that Trey and Taylor were lovers, that they were having their differences, and that they asked Johnson if they could use the roof to talk. Once on the roof, a quarrel broke out during which they both accidentally fell off of the roof and died. Quite a brilliant plan, if I do say so myself."

The senior police officer said, "It might have been a brilliant plan if the lady here did not have this recording. But seeing that she does, I am going to have to place you under arrest."

The senior officer said to the junior officer, "Cuff Mr. Sinclair and his four security guards. We will take them downstairs. On our way, we will round up the two guards who were sent to the young lady's house from the janitor's closet.

"We will take all seven of them to the front of the building. We'll let the coroner handle the decedent. We will load Mr. Sinclair and the two wounded security guards into the ambulance. You will ride with them to the hospital.

"I will take the two remaining security guards from the roof and the two security guards from the janitor's closet to the station."

The coroner loaded Trey's dead body into his vehicle. Mr. Sinclair and the two wounded guards, Johnson and Hank, went in the ambulance with the junior officer.

The senior officer loaded the two guards from the roof and the two guards from the janitor's closet into his police van and joined everyone in front of the building.

The two receptionists and the three guards from the first-floor security room remained.

The senior officer advised them that if they had given all of their information to the junior officer and signed their joint statement, they were free to go. They were relieved. They all left quickly.

The senior officer took the four guards to the police station.

Taylor, Amanda, Moose, Bart, and Rick left in the Suburban. Lester drove his van. He took Dave, and they all went to Amanda's.

Once at Amanda's, I thanked Moose, Bart, Lester, and Dave profusely. We were going to discuss what we knew, but we were all too tired. Moose, Bart, Lester, and Dave left in Lester's van.

Taylor and I spoke with Amanda. We asked her if she would like to come and stay with us as we were not certain whether Sinclair's arrangements for her were complete. She declined. It didn't appear as if he would have had an opportunity to make other arrangements. She wanted to stay home and sleep in her own bed.

Taylor was equally anxious to get home, as was I.

Taylor and I drove the Suburban to our house, parked, and went inside. It felt good to be home. We left Taylor's car at her office.

There would be much legal stuff, but we were not going to face it tonight.

Chapter Thirty-Three
The Street Crimes

After a couple days of rest, Rick and Taylor went back to business as usual. Rick, of course, could not prosecute the case against Sinclair as he would be a witness. The prosecution would take place in Lakeside, the situs of the crime, and he did not work in that office anyway.

During the next several weeks, Sinclair as arraigned. He pleaded not guilty. Though he was considered a flight risk and though the charge was first degree murder, he was still able to get bail. He had to surrender his passport.

Johnson, Hank, Phil, and Jose were released in one way or another. The Lakeside DA made a deal with Jose. Jose would testify against Sinclair in exchange for the much-reduced crime of trespassing. He would be released OR, and would pay a small fine. Though he had first-hand knowledge of what occurred, as he was present on the roof, he did not actually participate in the throwing operation.

Johnson and Hank, as the men who actually threw Trey and Taylor off of the roof, were looking at murder charges. With Phil, it was still uncertain. If he was willing to testify for the prosecution, he might be able to get his crime reduced to involuntary manslaughter.

The two guys who were hired to go to Amanda's remained in custody for a few days. At their arraignment, they pleaded no-contest to misdemeanor breaking and entering and were released for time served. The DA felt that after hearing the story of their interrogation, it was best to get them in and out of the system as quickly as possible.

The two receptionists and three security guards in the first-floor security room were lauded as heroes, as they should have been. The company was quick to mend its image by saying that these five employees saved the day by assisting in the apprehension of several dangerous felons, without, of course, mentioning that the CEO was one of those felons.

All five received cash rewards, raises, promotions, and premier parking spaces, all of which were richly deserved.

Chapter Thirty-Four
Trials and Tribulations

Consider the prosecution of Paul Sinclair, former CEO of Allied Chemical. Mr. Sinclair learned that a deputy attorney general (Taylor Shaw) witnessed the illegal dumping of toxic waste by Allied and that this dumping caused the death of an Allied employee. Rather than doing damage control, Sinclair concocted a plan to kill the witness by throwing her from the roof of his office building and maintaining that it was an accident which occurred during a lover's quarrel.

Rather than just giving the order, he decided to deliver a short speech extolling his brilliance in coming up with such an artful plan.

Even this might have been reduced to a he said/she said side show except for the fact that the victim, Taylor Shaw, was able to record his speech revealing his acts and intentions with a miniature USB microphone, and the fact that Trey actually died.

In his speech, he callously stated that his actions were to maximize earnings to bolster stock price and that to dispose of the witness was for the greater good. His good.

He actually admitted to the crime when he said, "In a few minutes, I will have Hank throw Taylor from the roof to her certain death. I will have Johnson throw Trey from the roof."

During his plea and sentencing negotiations, Sinclair was quick to implicate John Deaver as a bad actor. As we know, Mr. Deaver was the head of the environmental section of the State Attorney General's Office in Sacramento. He was tasked by the Attorney General himself to develop an environmental task force with deputies located in offices scattered throughout the State. This was done to provide optimal coverage in places remote from the main office in Sacramento.

Taylor was selected to become a member of the task force and to remain in Fairview. Under normal circumstances, Deaver, who was really only interested in protecting violators, would never have selected Taylor. Her aggressive investigative techniques and painful honesty were well known throughout the State making her difficult to control. She wound up on the task force because she was selected by her boss, Mr. Patterson, who had much confidence in her and actually admired her methods, though he might not admit to it publicly. Also, she was a necessary component to an operation needing to demonstrate diversity as she was the only qualified woman.

Under Deaver's plan, which was brilliant, he would receive payoffs from various large corporations to keep tabs on any possible environmental law violations being investigated. He did this by having his task force members who he placed around the State report to him about their on-going investigations, which was actually their job. This would give him advanced knowledge of their plans to pursue any of his clients.

This would place Deaver in a position to provide to his clients with advanced knowledge of environmental investigations which would afford them the opportunity to correct or conceal the violations before getting caught.

When Taylor became too aggressive, Deaver sent Trey to the Fairview office to keep tabs on her and to dissuade her from investigating or acting against the interests of his corporate clients. The plan was a good one. Even the task force members did not know what Deaver was actually doing. Silly them, they actually thought that the task force was organized to improve the work of the AG's office. As a result, the task force members reported to Deaver openly and honestly.

Sinclair offered up Deaver in hopes of receiving a reduced sentence. It would be a rare case in which the court would hand down a sentence less than that contained in the statutory guide lines. However, in this case, the possible punishments are so severe, that anything would help. If by giving Deaver to the prosecution the death penalty could be taken off of the table, it would be well worth it, at least as far as Sinclair was concerned.

The case against Sinclair, Johnson, Hank, Phil, and Jose is compelling as it involves the felony murder rule, which was changed in California in 2019.

Traditionally, murder has been defined as the unlawful taking of a human life with malice. The term "malice" does not require that the person acted with ill will towards the victim will but only that he acted with wanton disregard for human life with a high degree of probability that his acts would result in death. Both first and second-degree murder require the existence of malice.

Traditionally, first degree murder has been defined as a murder that is willful, deliberate, or premeditated; is committed by poison, torture, or lying in wait; or is committed by explosives or weapons of mass destruction. All other murders are second degree murder.

Before the passage of the new felony murder law, a defendant could be convicted of first-degree murder when there was a death during the commission of a felony, even if the death was accidental, was unintentional, or the defendant had no knowledge of it.

In 2019, the new felony murder law was enacted by Senate Bill 1437. Under the new felony murder law, a defendant involved in the perpetration or attempted perpetration of a felony during which a death occurred would only liable for felony murder if (1) he was the actual killer; (2) he was not the actual killer, but with intent to kill, aided, abetted, counseled, commanded, induced, solicited, requested, or assisted the actual killer in the commission of murder; (3) he was a major participant in the underlying felony and acted with reckless indifference to human life; or (4) an on-duty police officer was killed.

In other words, for a defendant to be guilty of felony murder, it was not enough that he was merely present at the crime, but he needed to have intent kill or show reckless indifference to human life. This was the case even if the attempted felony was unsuccessful. If the killing was negligent or accidental, it was not felony murder.

The question of aiding and abetting is fairly complicated. In Anglo-American law, it has long been the rule that a person may be found guilty of the same crime as the perpetrator if he aids or abets in its commission, even if he did not participate in it directly. This concept was codified in Penal Code Section 31.

Even after the new felony murder law, it is still the case that someone may be found guilty of murder for aiding and abetting. SB 1437 does not eliminate all murder liability for aiders and abettors. However, under the new felony murder law, for the crime of an aider or abettor to rise to the level of a felony murder, it must be shown that the defendant not only aided and abetted but that he aided and abetted with the intent to kill or that he acted with reckless indifference to human life.

The new felony murder law somewhat expands the definition of first-degree murder for murders committed during felonies. Under the new felony murder law, a felony murder is considered first degree murder if death occurs during the commission or attempted commission of one of the listed dangerous felonies including: arson, rape, carjacking, kidnapping, torture, burglary, robbery, mayhem, or certain sex acts. No additional proof of first-degree murder is required.

All murders that are not premeditated or are not committed during one of the listed felonies is not first-degree murder but is second degree murder.

The importance of the distinction between first and second-degree murder may be seen in sentencing. Murder in the first degree carries a sentence of death, life without the possibility of parole, or imprisonment for 25 years to life. Murder in the second degree carries a sentence of 15 years to life, unless a peace officer is involved.

A distinction should be noted between felony murder and involuntary manslaughter.

Felony murder requires an intent to kill, whereas manslaughter is defined by a lack of intent. Felony murder requires a felony to be committed or attempted in connection with the killing of another person, whereas manslaughter can be committed during an otherwise legal act.

Chapter Thirty-Five
Sinclair, Trey, and Deaver

Sinclair was in very bad shape legally. He admitted to premeditation in his speech on the roof, and the speech was recorded.

Sinclair did not actually kill anyone, but he did order the killings. He has liability for first degree murder for aiding and abetting notwithstanding the new felony murder law, as he acted with intent to kill or, at very least, reckless indifference to human live.

A person is guilty of implied malice if by words or conduct he intentionally encourages the perpetrator to commit an act naturally dangerous to human life with knowledge of the perpetrator's intent. Sinclair, as the master mind of the entire enterprise, would certainly be found to have aided or abetted the crime with intent to kill, even by his own admission.

SB 1437 does not eliminate murder liability for aiders and abettors, but aiders and abettors may be convicted of first-degree premeditated murder based on aiding and abetting principles, so long as the requisite intent or indifference may be shown.

As we know, Sinclair offered up Deaver to try to avoid the death penalty. He was willing to take a plea to try to get 25 to life rather than death or life without the possibility of parole. He would be a model prisoner, and he could serve fewer than 25 years and could arrange for house arrest or work furlough if he could make his deal.

Trey was now deceased. He did commit an assault and battery against Taylor and did falsely imprison and kidnap her. It is difficult to say whether he intended for all of the bad things that happened to her to actually occur. One could argue that he was just a useful idiot, which though true, is not a defense.

Trey's criminal liability is somewhat moot as he died before he could be charged with a crime. When he saw that Taylor witnessed not only the illegal dumping but also the death of an Allied employee, he made the decision to knock her out and work out a plan with Deaver to determine what would be done with her.

When Trey telephoned Deaver, Deaver telephoned Sinclair. Sinclair told Deaver to have Trey take her to the Allied building.

In California, a person is under no legal duty to report a crime, and failure to report a crime is generally not a crime itself, unless the person is a mandated reporter. If Deaver had disregarded Trey's request, he may have had no legal duty to report a crime.

However, after he learned that a felony had been committed, if he aided the principal with the intent that the principal would avoid arrest and punishment, he would be liable as an accessory after the fact under Penal Code Section 32.

Deaver would be an accessory after the fact to Taylor's battery and kidnapping. At this point, the plan to kill her was not known to Trey or Deaver or, perhaps, even to Sinclair.

If Deaver and Tray discovered that Sinclair intended to murder Taylor and if Deaver or Trey encouraged, facilitated, or promoted that offense, they might be considered aiders and abettors in Taylor's murder which would make them liable for the same criminal charges as the direct perpetrator under Penal Code Section 31.

(Under our present law, there is no longer accessory before the fact liability. An accessory before the fact may now be considered an aider and abettor and, as such, is liable for the same crime as the actual perpetrator.)

The facts show that the murder plan was that of Sinclair's. There was no particular evidence that Trey or Deaver facilitated him with that plan.

Taylor could have pressed a civil case against Trey's estate, but he would not have sufficient assets to satisfy a judgment. She would sue Trey's employer for civil damages for its failure to protect her.

For his part, Deaver would lose his law license, which loss he richly deserved. He maintained that he only wanted Trey to keep an eye on Taylor and Amanda so that they would not get hurt by any of the thugs hired by the large corporations they were investigating. He turned things around to make it appear as if he was doing something good.

The fact that Trey died gave him room to make up the story that he did not know what Trey was doing or planning to do with Taylor, or for whom Trey was working, even though he was actually working for him.

Sinclair's contention that Deaver supplied him with information about investigations by the Attorney General's Office boiled down to his word against Sinclair's.

The word of Sinclair, a convicted murderer, did not carry much weight, but was enough to maintain an administrative judgment against Deaver's law license.

Chapter Thirty-Six
Johnson, Hank, Phil, and Jose

Johnson was the actual perpetrator of a murder, the murder of Trey. He might claim that he lacked malice. Penal Code Section 188 states that malice may be implied when circumstances show an abandoned and malignant heart, certainly the case with Johnson.

The prosecutor might argue that the killing was a felony murder and that it occurred during the commission of a felony listed in PC 190, i.e., kidnapping, making the killing first degree murder without a further showing.

When relying on the commission of a felony it must be remembered that all of the elements of the underlying crime must be proven. Kidnapping requires moving the victim a substantial distance. For example, moving a person from one side of a room to the other does not provide movement sufficient for a kidnapping or for a felony murder based on kidnapping.

At the site, Taylor was moved from Three Palms to the cage and from the cage to the roof. The defense will argue that the movement was not sufficient for kidnapping or felony murder and that the other movement, done by Trey, was not sanctioned by Johnson or Sinclair.

Hank committed roughly the same transgression as Johnson. The only difference was that since Taylor survived, Hank's actions constituted an attempt. For the purposes of the felony murder rule, an attempt is treated the same as a completed crime.

As an accomplice, the prosecution would argue that Hank possessed malice aforethought as throwing someone off of a 15-story building shows an abandoned and malignant heart.

Phil did not throw anyone off of a building. As an accomplice, he might argue that he had no knowledge of the plan and did not wish to put either Trey or Taylor in a position to be thrown off of the building.

With respect to felony murder, Phil could argue that the underlying felony of kidnapping was not completed. He could also argue that he was not a major participant in the underlying felony.

Jose had roughly the same arguments as Phil. As the case against Jose was the weakest, the DA made a deal with him that he would testify against Sinclair, Johnson, Hank, and Phil in exchange for a light sentence.

Chapter Thirty-Seven
The Environmental Crimes And Return to Normalcy

Mr. Sinclair allowed his ego to get in his way. If he had reported the illegal dumping and the unfortunate death, he would have lost his position, some of his possessions, and, perhaps, would have even spent some time in jail.

However, he considered the risk of killing Trey and Taylor to be a better alternative than losing his lifestyle.

Some of his thinking may have been influenced by recent trends in CEO appraisal. Consider an article in The Conversation written by Chelsea Liu.

The article states, "... new research shows that the chief executives of companies sued for environmental wrongdoing commonly suffer little reputational damage."

The article goes on to say that civil liability of a CEO is generally covered by the company's insurance and that criminal prosecutions are rare due to burden of proof problems.

Attention was then directed to market-based penalties – those imposed by the collective actions of several corporations.

The conclusion reached was that "there is no evidence to suggest that individual CEOs are punished by impaired reputation, when their companies have been embroiled in environmental allegations."

Clearly, if the allegation had been simply illegal dumping without the attendant death of an employee, coming clean would have been the clear path. A death changes much, but the punishment for death in these circumstances is so lenient that admission may still have been the better course.

The facts in the Sinclair case are nearly the same as those in the Port Arthur case. In Port Arthur, an employee involved in illegal dumping died as a result of exposure to hydrogen sulfide, the same poisonous gas which caused the death in Sinclair's case. The highest-ranking corporate officer admitted that he did not properly protect the deceased employees from exposure to the deadly gas.

That officer was sentenced to 12 months in federal prison for violating the Occupational Safety and Health Act (OSHA) and payment of a $5,000.00 fine.

If the legal system remained true to form, as it generally does, Sinclair might have been let off with 12 months in federal prison and a $5,000.00 fine. Though this would have been embarrassing, would have meant prison food and lodging for a year, and would have meant not living in luxury with a beautiful wife, it would have been better than the 25 years to life that he will probably be serving, the unnecessary death of Trey, and the exposure of Taylor to frightening conditions, treatment, and near death.

After her ordeal, Taylor took a couple of days off to recuperate. It was still hot in the desert, and she and Rick drove over to the coast and stayed in Del Mar in north San Diego county for a couple of days just enjoying the beach, the weather, the food, the hotel, and each another.

Over the next months, the various actors learned their respective fates.

Sinclair pleaded guilty to first degree murder but received the most lenient sentence available, 25 years to life. He would be eligible for parole in a probably fewer than a dozen years.

Deaver pleaded guilty to being an accessory after the fact to Taylor's kidnapping, a felony, lost his law license, was fired from the AG's office, and was subject to various lawsuits. Future employment for him will be difficult.

Taylor received a promotion. She was now head of the environmental services department for the entire southern half of California. Her boss, Mr. Patterson, would remain head of the Fairview office. He was shown to have had no knowledge of the Sinclair-Deaver-Trey alliance, with which Taylor agreed.

She was a perfect choice for the job. As is well known, federal and State criminal, civil, and administrative enforcement often overlap. Most federal environmental statutes allow the federal government to conduct both civil and criminal investigations, initiate both civil and criminal proceedings, and seek both civil and criminal sanctions.

Many statutes authorize States to administer federal regulations which grants to the federal and State governments concurrent civil and criminal enforcement authority.

Many States have enacted environmental laws that grant State officials both civil and criminal enforcement power. Some statutes and State common law allow private plaintiffs to sue private parties for environmental violations.

The exercise of these powers often subjects defendants to parallel and successive proceedings that present significant substantive and procedural problems, making their legal ordeal worse than expected.

Taylor's strong suit was working with people. Her interest was in achieving a result that would best protect the interests of citizens.

Allied was also fined for Sinclair's environmental violations.

Taylor sued Allied for her imprisonment and near death. They were more than happy to pay her a $600,000. settlement. She and Rick put this money away for a new house, when the time came. She probably would have received 3 million if she had gone to trial.

Ultimately, Johnson and Hank pleaded to second degree murder. Phil cooperated as well as he could. For this, he was rewarded with a plea to involuntary manslaughter, which carries a four-year maximum.

Jose, whose testimony, along with the tape, made it all possible pleaded to misdemeanor trespassing with a small fine (which Taylor paid for him in cash.) She actually like him and enjoyed talking to him while she was in the cage.

Rick continued his work with the Haven DA. The only other places he could go would be into private practice, political office, or the bench. For now, he would stay where he was, senior trial deputy.

Chapter Thirty-Eight
Taylor and Amanda

Taylor and Amanda continued both their friendship and their close working relationship. Amanda was like a little sister. She came to Taylor for all types of advice. Taylor tried to explain to her that her own experience with men was so limited that she felt unqualified to give advice in that department.

Amanda reminded her that her quick thinking about Trey was of great benefit. But Taylor reminded her that she too misjudged him, allowing him to come with her to Three Palms, where he knocked her out and took her to the cage.

Taylor and Amanda worked several interesting cases. They vowed to be tough but fair. Taylor realized that commerce was necessary and tried to protect the environment within the framework of encouraging enterprise.

Taylor reasoned that if the companies were going to take chances breaking the law, they would have to clean up their act and pay fines accordingly, as the money from the fines was often used to make the injured parties whole.

Taylor and Amanda decided that criminal sanctions would be imposed as often as possible to make certain that the violators kept their promises.

Rick was very pleased that Taylor had such a deep friendship with Amanda. During the years that he has known her, he worried that she might never learn to trust anyone enough to develop a true friendship. The Amanda relationship was a good thing.

Chapter Thirty-Nine
One Year Anniversary

Rick and Taylor had been married a year, and the day had come when they would celebrate their one-year anniversary.

They selected their favorite restaurant. Rick made a reservation for 7:30, and, of course, arrived early. He was shown to their favorite table in the back of the room. They were both working, so they drove separately. Taylor was running late as she wanted to finish work and go home to change before their reservation.

At 7:45 Rick could see Taylor enter the restaurant and make her way to the hostess station. She followed the hostess down into the dining room.

She looked so spectacularly beautiful that Rick gasped. Everyone in the room was looking at her, including the women.

She came over to the table; Rick stood.

She asked, "May I sit?"

Rick replied, "Certainly. I'm sorry."

She sat down, and they engaged in some small talk. After a few minutes, Rick said, "I'm so sorry that you had to go through this whole ordeal with Sinclair and Allied Chemical. I feel terrible that you were put in such a horrible position. You must have been so worried that you would not make it out of there alive."

She replied, as only she could, "I wasn't worried."

Rick responded, "Not worried. How can that be?"

She answered, "Because I knew that you would come for me."

About the Author

Tighe Taylor, JD is a graduate of Whittier College, School of Law, located in Los Angeles County. He lives and works in Los Angeles, where he owns and operates a real estate inspection firm and practices law and financial planning. His prior literary works include *The Tragic Death of Marina Habe*, a true crime account of the most unfortunate kidnapping and murder of Marina Habe, a childhood friend, and *The Kidnapping of Tammy Fitzgerald*, a work of crime fiction.

www.ingramcontent.com/pod-product-compliance
Lightning Source LLC
LaVergne TN
LVHW041704060526
838201LV00043B/576